THE

AWAKENING

J.R. HASTEY

Printed in the United States of America

First Printing, 2017

Title ID: 6658255

ISBN-13: 978-1539633297

Acknowledgements

I would like to thank my family and friends for encouraging me to write this book. It has been an experience and I hope the readers enjoy my story. I would also like to especially thank Melissa and Christopher for helping me and doing everything you have done.

CHAPTER 1

Let me start off by giving you a little insight about myself. My name is Eric Summers, I'm nineteen with average, slightly toned build, dark wavy hair and brown eyes. I'm not ugly by any means, just average. I grew up in a small town in the Texas Panhandle from the age of four until I was almost eighteen. I had a great relationship with my mom, but could not wait to grow up and be on my own. I learned pretty fast that momma knew a lot more than I thought she did.

You see, I always had a hard time in school, not with academics per say, but more with the other kids my age. I was never bullied or anything like that, but most definitely got picked on a lot. As I got older, I basically just learned to fade into the background and become invisible. Don't feel sorry for me though, this isn't a pity or sob story, being invisible is how I preferred it and at times, I still do.

I decided at an early age that I was going to hit the road as soon as I could and move to the big city, all the fancy lights and people everywhere, it would be like a dream come true to me, so shortly after my sixteenth birthday I decided I was going to make plans and move out on my own to make that dream a reality.

However, with me... Let me just put it this way, planning ahead was never my strong suit. I do try to prepare for the future, but it always backfires or I just get let down.

So, I figured, what the hell, just go for it, let's see where the journey takes me, just spread my wings and fly free.

That's about the time, I splatter head first into an oncoming windshield.

SPLAT!

You see, people always think I'm joking, but I'm dead serious, if it weren't for bad luck, then I'd have no luck at all and that's no joking matter!

I would love to find the person that I pissed off, who has my voodoo doll, apologize profusely and beg them to take the needles out.

The only thing that got me through all the adolescent B.S. was Collin. Collin Grainger, my best friend and hero since we were little kids. If I could count on nothing else, I could count on him.

He was always there for me whenever I needed him to be. He would always stick up for me and protect me, no matter what others might say, he was a true friend and those are hard to come by nowadays.

I can recall several occasions where someone was picking on me or giving me a hard time and he would come out of nowhere making them back off.

Collin was always popular and it didn't take much for people to do as he said and when he told people to leave me alone, they pretty much did, at least for the time being.

We always said that we would be friends and that we would stick together forever and we even planned on attending the same college and starting a business together one day.

At times, it was hard to be his friend, people always said that he was the cute one, the funny one, the smart one, the athletic one and the list goes on forever.

Not that I'm jealous, okay maybe I am a little jealous. At the same time, it made me feel good, of all the people in the world, Collin chose me to be his best friend. That had always made me feel special, like for once in my life, something good was actually happening to me.

I suppose I can't deny that the accusations about him were true though, Collin has always been tall and slender with a swimmer's build, muscular back and shoulders, with abs to boot. It doesn't hurt his appearance any, that he has the typical blonde hair, blue eyes and chiseled face.

Collin was the football, track, basketball, and any other extra-curricular activity's star, not the typical dumb high school jock though, he had a great personality as well, he was smart, funny, kind, caring, and this list too, goes on and on. I guess that is why I always loved him, he was like a brother to me, my protector, my everything.

Then here I am, hating sports, but of course I went to stand on the sidelines and cheer him on, after all, he was my rock so it was the least I could do.

I always got along with people, but like I said, I usually preferred to stand in the shadows, so of course it never bothered me that it was Collin's shadow I got to stand in.

Any time someone gave me any trouble, he was always right there to defend me. Collin was always running to my rescue, I needed a lot of rescuing, it was more of a full-time job for him and he somehow always made me feel comfortable, just him being there could take the edge off just about any situation.

The closest to sports I ever cared to get to was dancing. I loved to dance as did Collin, we planned on attending a performing arts school and opening our own studio someday.

Collin was an amazing dancer; he was very elegant with perfect form and surefooted. I suppose all the sports were good for something.

I am not too bad of a dancer myself, however unlike Collin, I am more of what people call a free-spirited dancer. We have a perfect balance between our two styles.

We were always the center of attention when we would go to the school dances and other events. That's about the only time I could care less what everyone else thought of me.

However, Collin seemed to love being in the limelight, it was almost as if this is where he belonged.

We loved to flaunt our dance moves and on occasion, we would even choreograph a few routines together, just to show off a little.

Our senior year has just flown by, for that I am grateful. I'm so ready to leave high school behind and begin our new adventure.

Now my eighteenth birthday was just around the corner and as per usual, I was so unprepared. We also graduate in a few months and we were still planning on attending the same college together.

All I had to do was stick it out a little while longer and we could leave the small town living and move in to our own dorm or maybe even rent an apartment together.

The excitement was almost overwhelming, my new adventure was finally about to begin. If only I had known how much of an adventure it would be.

CHAPTER 2

Graduating was a lot harder than I thought. The more excited I got to leave this life behind, the more I knew I would miss it, with Collin being my only friend, school would not be hard to leave.

However, the hardest part will be leaving my parents behind. As I said, my mother and I have always been close. She will be the one that I miss the most, I think she is mostly happy for me, however I know she will miss me as well.

We spent the last few weeks with our parents and going over memories of when we were little. The nostalgic memories flowing back to me like a hurricane down memory Lane.

Summer was here and high school was behind us now and we were one step closer to adulthood or that's what I liked to tell myself anyway.

Summers were always my favorite time of year. I usually got invited to go with Collin and his parents on their vacations, it was always lavish hotels with room service and rooftop swimming pools, shopping galore and the most expensive restaurants.

Then after we got back from where ever his parents had taken us, they needed to rest at one of their lake houses. It must be tiring to be that rich, I wouldn't know the feeling. I always had everything I ever needed growing up, but Collin always had everything that he needed and wanted as well.

This summer was even better, my parents got to come along, so we just made it a family event. Our parents were pretty close too, in fact, they were the whole reason we moved here in the first place. My dad works for Collin's father and they went to the same college, so it was no surprise when my dad got the call to come work for his company. After we returned from vacation, Collin and I spent the summer pretty much as we had every summer before, most of which was spent at his house.

It was pretty much like every child's dream and now that we were getting older, it was even better. We spent the days hanging out by the pool getting a tan, taking a dip to cool off. The cooler evenings we spent hanging out in the hot tub and on rainy days, we would usually try to come up with some indoor activity like playing video games or whatever else we could think of.

I wasn't crazy over playing video games, but it was something that Collin really enjoyed, so of course I would play along. My favorite days were the sunny days of course, watching Collin lay out in the sun, getting a tan. Watching him glisten in the sun, with nothing more than a speedo on. He would sometimes ask me to put suntan lotion on his back for him, I loved this most of all, as I said before, he did have a great body.

Not that I didn't have a good body too, but Collin had a certain confidence about him, that let you know that he knew he had a great body and he enjoyed when people looked at him. That's probably about the only vein thing about him, he was pretty and he knew it.

I had a great physique, but I lacked his confidence and that made a big difference. Collin would walk around naked, if he thought he could get away with it.

Other days we would just lounge around, enjoying each other's company, rather we were in deep conversation or just enjoying the silence together.

Collin was the easiest person in the world to talk to, besides the fact that we had known each other for nearly our entire lives. He pretty much already knew everything there was to know about me, as I too knew just about everything about him. We knew each other's silly little quirks, what the other liked to eat or drink, and sometimes we would even finished each other's sentences. For us being so completely and entirely different and coming from two separate lifestyles, it was a little scary how much we were alike.

Collin was always popular in school, but he never really had any other friends to speak of other than me.

Of course, he was invited to all the cool kids houses for sleepovers and birthday parties, but if I couldn't go, he would stay home and hang out with me. I think we both preferred it that way.

Our parents, on the other hand, I'm sure thought it was a little weird, they would try to encourage us to seek out other friendships, but by the time we were in our teens, I think they finally gave up on the idea of us being separated.

This summer was a little different because we had to prepare for college. We had to pack all our belongings and spend as much time with our parents as we could before be leaving on our new adventure.

As I sat there packing my stuff I started to think about all the things I was going to miss most, like shopping with my mom, just spending time with her all together.

We were so close, we used to do everything together. I started to feel tears building up in my eyes. I am going to miss my mom, but at the same time I am more than ready to be on my own or at least that's what I thought anyway!

As Friday got closer, like normal, I was scrambling to get everything ready. I know it's hard to believe, but I had of course procrastinated. So here I was just throwing anything and everything I owned in to boxes so I could be ready for Collin to pick me up.

Our parents had begged us to let them take us to college, but like typical teenagers, we refused the offer. It wasn't like we were going all that far, it was only four hours away, I knew we could handle the trip alone. We were adults, somewhat, we don't need our parents to help us. We can do this, or at least that's what I would tell myself!

As per usual, Collin was right on time to pick me up, another way we were so completely different, he was always so punctual if not early and I was always late. My own mother has always said that I would even be late to my own funeral, she's probably right about that too.

We threw my very few boxes in with Collins, said our goodbyes, and headed to the unknown life of college students.

I'm surprised my mom didn't try to follow us to the college however, I'm sure the thought probably did cross her mind. My dad, undoubtedly had to hide the car keys from her to keep her from doing it, that thought did make me smile though, at the same time it made me a little sadder.

I leaned out the passenger side window and waved my goodbyes to our parents. As we drove off, I flipped down the vanity mirror and watched them getting smaller and smaller, till I could no longer see them. I returned the mirror and fought back the tears, as we headed off into the unknown.

We got to the college early for admissions. Even though it was only a short four-hour drive from home, we were anxious to start our adventure. Plus, we wanted to get there early to unpack and get everything situated.

We couldn't get a dorm together so Collin's parents rented us a little apartment off campus and it was only a couple blocks from the college, which was a good thing, since I still didn't have a car.

All Collin had to do was smile and bat his eyes at his parents and they faltered to his every whim, as does everyone else for that matter, myself included.

Collin got a brand-new car for his sixteenth birthday and got another brand-new car for his eighteenth. I'm surprised his parents didn't have it wrapped in a big red bow.

It really was a wonder that Collin didn't turn out to be one of those spoiled little rich kids with a complex that the world owes them a favor and everything should be handed to them. I suppose that's another thing that makes him so great, he has always appreciated everything he has, no matter how hard his parents tried to turn him into the perfect little Stepford child, he has always been himself and stayed true to that.

At one point his parents even tried to make him go off to some fancy prep school, but he refused to leave me and talked them into letting him stay in the public-school system.

I'm sure they absolutely loved that, but they got over it, just like they always did, but I'm sure the thought of their only son attending a public school, was simply mortifying to them.

I suppose I can't complain too much, I would have just died had he gone half way across the world to attend school, so it worked out for me too, as did everything else, like the new cars, I guess I too got to reap the benefits of his spoils.

I was also glad they got us the apartment, as I was dreading living in the dorms, the whole community bathroom just wasn't my thing and I looked forward to a bath from time to time, which obviously wouldn't be possible in the dorms. Now that I think about it, I suppose I should probably send his parents a thank you letter.

We pulled up to our little two-bedroom apartment and started to unload. Even as tiny as it was, it was like a mansion for me. I was finally free of the chains of small town living.

For the first time in what seemed like forever, I could breathe, I felt like I could finally be myself for once in my life and not have to live up to the standards of everyone else or at least what they thought I should be.

CHAPTER 3

Collin brought in all the heavy boxes as I started to unpack them. I had to keep pausing, just to smile and look around. I took my shoes off at the front door and let my toes sink into the thick beige and tan speckled carpet, the sensation tingling up through the bottom of my feet to the top of my head.

I could still smell the freshly painted taupe and eggshell colored walls. The apartment looked plain, yet had a very elegant and welcoming feel to it as well.

Homey, that's what it was, it was my first home away from home. I closed my eyes and envisioned what it would look like all put together, I couldn't wait to get everything set up.

As I opened my eyes and looked around, I realized that the apartment was not quite as small as I had first thought.

Coming through the front door off to the right is the dining room, connected to that is the kitchen, with a counter bar top dividing the kitchen from the living room. Then to the left is the living room and down the short hallway, on the left is the bathroom and at the end of the hallway are the bedrooms. Right across the hall, that's where Collin will be.

I don't think I have ever felt so safe either. Now instead of having to call or text him and wait till the next day to see him, he will be right there, so close.

That night we got almost everything unpacked and put away. Mine was easy with my whopping two whole boxes and some clothes. Collin, on the other hand had a lot more things.

Collin knew that I didn't have much of the needed things to live on my own, he and his parents made sure that we wouldn't be without.

I was almost embarrassed when I was unpacking, all Collin's boxes where neatly packed and labeled, while mine looked like an 'everything's half off' box at a garage sale or something that had been picked through and tossed aside.

We got most of the things put together and hung up or put in its right place and the movers put all our furniture together and set it up for us. The apartment was really starting to come together, so we decide to finish for the night, order a pizza, catch a movie, then turn in early.

As I laid there trying to go to sleep, I tossed and turned for what seemed like an eternity, the excitement still surging through my body, so I figured I might as well get up and take a nice hot bath to help me relax, then maybe I could get some sleep.

I know it may sound childish, but I still like to take a bubble bath from time to time. I turned on the water and adjusted it to the perfect temperature, added my bubbles, lit some candles and turned out the lights.

I stuck one toe into the water first, to test the temperature, it was hot so I just slowly eased the rest of my body in. The hot water felt so wonderful, I think I could physically feel the energy seeping out of my pores.

I hadn't realized how sore I really was, it must have been from all the lifting and unpacking, I wasn't used to manual labor. I wrung out my steaming hot rag and threw it over my eyes, cleared my thoughts and just as I was about to doze off, I heard a faint knock on the door.

"Eric, are you in there?" Collin asked.

"Yes! If you need to use the bathroom I can leave!" I replied, so startled that I sat up in the tub too quickly and sloshed water everywhere.

"No, it's quite alright. We are two guys living in a one bathroom apartment. Can I just come in?" He asked sounding a little irritated.

I could tell by the sound of his voice that something was wrong. I leaned back again in the tub and quickly covered myself with the rag.

"Um, sure?" I said uneasily.

"Besides, it's not like I haven't seen you naked before." He said teasingly, as he walked in and closed the door behind him.

As Collin turned toward me, I could see in the candlelight that he only had on his underwear and nothing else. My heart seemed to skip a beat. In the dim light, his muscular body looked even more like a Greek statue. His rippled abs were like a washboard that seemed to pulsate with the dancing light, adding the perfect amount of highlight and contour in the shadows as he slowly walked over to me.

My eyes drifted down his body to his happy trail peeking out through the top of his underwear. I looked down at my rag to make sure it was still covering me. My groin felt all tingly as I shook my head to clear my thoughts and tried to ignore the throbbing between my thighs.

Thank god, I remembered to pack bubbles, is all I could think.

We had taken hundreds of baths together, but not since we were little and not in such an intimate setting.

Not to mention, it was a little different now that we were no longer kids. I think once puberty hits, it is a little inappropriate for people to take baths together.

Although, I suppose we did still take showers together, but only in the locker room, just like everyone else did in athletics. That was the norm and had been forever. I don't really know why it was so awkward for me now or why I was being so shy around him?

He has seen me naked many times before. Why are you acting like this? Snap out of it.

Once again, I cleared my thoughts and smiled at him as he walked over to the side of the tub, hoping that he wouldn't be able to see my bulging excitement hiding under the rag.

Chapter 4

He didn't even use the bathroom, he just sat down on the floor by the tub and looked at me.

"Um, are you okay?" I asked him, awkwardly trying to avoid eye contact.

"Yes. I... I just didn't... I just didn't want to be alone right now if that's okay?" He managed to stammer.

"Of course that's okay." I assured him, forgetting the awkwardness and looking at him with concern.

He seemed very dejected, which is out of character for him. I guess he could see the worry written all over my face.

"I'm fine, really. I'm glad you are here with me." He said, finally smiling at me.

"Me too." is all I could mutter, returning the smile.

We sat in silence for a moment. Which was surprisingly comfortable. Collin always had a way of making people feel comfortable in just about any situation. Even me being naked and vulnerable, sitting in my bubble bath like a two-year-old. I knew I didn't have to worry because Collin would never judge me.

"Here, lean up and I'll wash your back. I can at least do that if I'm going to just sit here." he said after a long pause.

He stood up and removed his underwear, then stepped in the tub with me and sat on the edge with his feet in the water.

"The water feels amazing." He said. Gliding his fingers through the water and scooping up a handful of bubbles.

I was petrified, too afraid to move, half in panic, my heart was fluttering so fast, I thought I might have a heart attack.

"What are you doing?" He chuckled as he gently gave my shoulder a nudge. "Scoot up."

I stiffened, in more ways than one, I didn't know what to say. My whole body seemed to be set ablaze, like a fiery tingle. I got a lump in my throat the size of a golf ball.

Even if I could have spoken, I don't know what I would have said to him. Since I didn't know what to say, I scooted toward the front of the tub, reluctantly handed him the rag that was currently in use to hide my erection and leaned forward to hug my knees, in hopes that it would better conceal my, now partially exposed secret beneath the bubbles.

The thought of fear and panic swept over me with more intensity, if that was even possible, as I felt him ease his body down into the hot water with me, each of his legs brushing both sides of my hips as he slid deeper in the hot bubbly water.

He placed his hands on my shoulders and I tensed.

"Relax." He said with a soft whisper.

His big hands were surprisingly soft as he lathered my back with soap. Chills ran up and down my spine as he wrung out the steaming hot rag and placed it gently on my back. He softly massaged the soap to a fizzy froth. The smell of lavender and coconut oil tickled my senses.

It was a weird sensation for me, even though I did love Collin, it was only as a friend, but his hands felt wonderful rubbing slowly up and down my back.

The confusing awkwardness was quickly wiped away with the soap as he once again wrung the hot rag over my shoulders, letting the water trickle down my body. I shivered, not from cold, but from the warm water droplets slowly sliding downward like hundreds of little tongues.

My eyes closed and I relaxed as my aching muscles were less tense now. I had no room for the awkward shyness, I was in a pure state of nirvana. Safe and sound, I always felt so safe around him.

He finished washing my back for me then he pulled me back into him and rested his chin on the top of my head while he wrapped his arms around my chest. I had never felt so relaxed and comfortable in all my life.

As I leaned back on him, I could feel his penis pressed against my back and yet, not even that seemed to bother me. I crossed my arms over his and he caressed my chest as he swaddled me and we again just sat in silence for a long while however, not long enough. He kissed the top of my head and stood up.

"Thanks for letting me sit with you a while." He said as he gently squeezed my shoulders and stepped out of the tub.

"Of course, Collin. If you ever need anything, all you have to do is ask." I said awkwardly as he toweled off and put his underwear back on.

"Goodnight Eric, see you in the morning." He said, smiling sweetly, before walking out and closing the door behind him.

Well, if I wasn't awake before, I sure as shit was now. I wasn't totally sure what the hell had just happened. I couldn't have been dreaming, I was completely and utterly confused and most definitely awake.

I had never had those kinds of thoughts about Collin, I mean yeah, he was attractive, but what the hell was that! Why had my body reacted that way towards him?

I totally submerged myself in the now cooling water and held my breath for as long as I could before coming up for air, then submerging again.

The thought of Collin's hands touching me, kept coming back. The more I tried to forget it, so my erection would go away, the stronger they got. I knew then, that I had to do something to get rid of this ache, the throbbing ache between my thighs, so did what I had done many times before and relieved myself, only this time I thought of Collin and what it felt like to have his hands touching all over my body. Believe me when I say, it didn't take long.

Then I soaked a few minutes more and decided the water had cooled too much, pulled the plug and watched as the water swirled slowly down the drain. I cleaned myself off, carefully stood up, towel dried, put on my favorite undies, brushed my teeth and headed to bed. Surely, I would be able to go to sleep now.

Chapter 5

The following morning, I woke to the smell of bacon and eggs cooking and the clattering of pots and pans. Collin is an excellent chef, but all I wanted to do was sleep some more.

Just five damn minutes, was that too much to ask for? I thought to myself angrily.

My hunger was stronger than the urge to sleep and the unyielding aroma was telling me, no forcing me to get up. I grumpily kicked the sheets off and swung my legs over the bed, rubbed the sleep out of my eyes and headed down the hallway to the source of the bouquet of breakfast foods and coffee.

"Well good morning sleepy head." Collin, too cheerful for morning said.

I gave him a contemptuous smirk and said, "Ha. Ha. Now where's my coffee?"

He just smiled and silently handed me the cup he had already prepared for me.

The perfect blend of bitter and sweet with the perfect amount of creamer over a perfect amount of ice.

PERFECTION.

I closed my eyes and inhaled so deeply that I could almost taste the coffee. I couldn't help, but smile.

"So, what would you like to do for our last two days of freedom?" Collin asked.

"Don't remind me. Two whole years of servitude! I'm down for anything." I said meekly. Now picking at my eggs.

"How about we check out the city? I read online that there are a few cool places to dance and I'm sure lots of people will be there with it being the last weekend before school starts." Collin asked.

"Sure. Sounds, um, cool." I laughed.

"Come on, who knows, you might even like it?" Collin teased.

"Maybe?" I said, shrugging my shoulders with indifference.

It was doubtful, as I said before, I really love to dance, but the whole crowded bar, just wasn't my thing. I could do without all the people.

However, I had never really been to an actual dance club so I might have been a little excited, but only a little.

We finished our breakfast and got dressed. As I was getting ready, I kept replaying last night over in my head.

Obviously, I just had an over active imagination.

He was just feeling homesick and didn't want to be alone, I told myself.

He was just being nice and knew my back hurt.

Everything seemed perfectly normal over breakfast. We had the same ol' banter we always did, nothing out of the ordinary, no awkward exchange, just perfectly happy.

I wasn't completely sure we would've had the same interaction at breakfast if Collin had known I had a monumental hard on last night?

I'm actually pretty sure that would have made things very awkward for the next two years. I am not completely convinced that he would even want to be my friend anymore, if he had known that I was so aroused. That, or he would just give me a hard time about it for the rest of my life. No pun intended.

Chapter 6

That evening we left to head out on our night on the town. We cruised around a while taking in all the sights. It was everything I had imagined and then some. All the lights and signs flickering and flashing advertisements, people everywhere walking around doing their own thing.

It was awesome.

We grabbed a bite to eat and finally pulled into Club 23 around 9:30, it was already hopping. You could hear the thump thump of the bass from outside. People were already lined up at the door waiting to get in, it was just like in the movies. My heart was pounding along with the beat of the music.

I guess I was a little more excited to experience the club scene than I had thought I would be. We waited our turn to get stamped and walk through the door. The lights were dim, but you could still see with the show of lasers, foggers and disco lights zooming around the bar.

The dance floor was crowded and there was an eclectic range of people dancing. The dance floor seemed to pulsate in rhythm with the beat of the music, almost as if it were a single organism swaying to the music, as opposed to individual people.

The floor was so crowded that it was hard to tell who was dancing with whom. Everyone was nearly touching arm to arm. I guess they were all pretty much dancing with each other.

Collin took me by the hand and drug me to the dance floor. We danced and swayed to the music, pretty much dancing with everyone in arm's length, bumping into one another, giggling and just moving to the sound and light show. It really was amazing, I was having the time of my life!

Collin seemed different that night, almost glowing. It could have been from all the lights flashing from the D.J. booth, but I don't think so. It was something else that I just couldn't quite figure it out. Maybe it was just all the excitement of the city or finally being able to be ourselves, but it was definitely something.

"What's wrong?" He asked. Pulling me out of my reverie.

"Nothing at all." I smiled. Leaning in closer so he could hear me, my lips almost brushing his ear as I started bouncing to the beat again.

"Want something to drink?" He shouted.

"What? I can't hear you." I yelled back.

Collin laughed and grabbed my hand, leading me off the dance floor toward the bar.

As we left the pulsating dance floor, weaving in and out of the crowd, we finally made it to the bar for some bottled water.

He yelled. "So! What do ya think?"

"Pretty cool!" I yelled back, still bobbing to the music.

"I really like it here." he said.

"Me too. I'm glad you brought me after all." I replied.

"See, I told you that you would like it! Come on, breaks over!" He shouted as he pulled me back to the dance floor.

Chapter 7

Everything was going great, we were in our own little world all by ourselves. Hundreds of people around, yet we seemed to be the only two people in the whole place. I guess that's why I accidentally bumped the guy behind me.

"I'm sorry." I said. Only halfway paying attention to whom I had just bumped in to.

"Watch what you're doing!" The excessively buff guy I bumped into said, as he pushed me back.

"I'm really sorry! I didn't mean to! I didn't even see you there." I said timidly.

"Maybe if you weren't all goo goo eyes with your boyfriend, you would have seen me!" He scolded, poking me in the chest.

"Hey! Easy man!" Collin interjected while shoving me aside to stand between the mountain and myself. "He's not my boyfriend, we are just friends. It's not like he meant to do it so calm down!" Collin ordered him.

"Maybe I'll whoop your ass too, right after I stomp his!" He exclaimed. Jutting his sausage like finger in my direction.

"Why don't you..."Collin started, but was interrupted by a fist to the jaw.

Collin flew back, knocking me over, which started a domino effect on the dance floor. People started falling and tripping over one another as they were slammed to the floor.

It was a hard blow, blood spattered across my face and with the momentum Collin's body hit mine, I wasn't sure at first, if the blood was mine or his.

Just then, a bouncer rushed over to save the day. I'm not sure how he had cut through the crowd so fast? He must have been watching before the whole ordeal even started.

"That's it Paul!" The burly bouncer shouted at the guy with a hell of a right hook. "You're out of here! This was your last warning!"

Obviously, the guy I accidentally bumped into was named Paul, 6' 4" every bit of 250 pounds of muscle, with tattoos covering both arms, he actually looked pretty scary, now that I had time to look at him.

"But..." Paul started to say, when he was interrupted again by the bouncer.

"OUT!" He said, pointing to the front exit as he followed Paul to the door.

I helped Collin get off the floor and by this time he had blood gushing from his nose.

I guess the blood was from him. I thought to myself.

Running to my rescue again, only to be injured. I suppose my bad luck rubbed off on him tonight. By the time Collin could get up, the music had cut off and everyone in the building was looking at us. I guided Collin to the bar and grabbed a handful of napkins just as the bouncer was heading back.

"You okay, kid?" He said obviously talking to Collin.

"Yeah, I don't think it's broken?" Collin replied with a nasally tone.

I would have laughed had it not been that I was so concerned.

"We've had problems with Paul before." The bouncer told us. "Tonight, was strike three. He won't be back in here again. So, you don't have to worry and sorry for your trouble. I'm Phil by the way."

"No worries and thank you for coming so fast!" I told Phil.

"I think I've had enough excitement for one night." Collin whined pleadingly, still stuffing his nose with napkins to control the bleeding.

"Okay." I told him as I grabbed another handful of napkins and led him out of the club.

Chapter 8

We made our way toward the exit as I said thank you once more to Phil and headed out for the car.

Phil was your normal bouncer type, bald head, with big arms, scruffy face, and the weight to back him up, had he ever got in a confrontation with anyone, but you could tell he had a sweet demeanor to him. I for one was just glad he was there.

We had to park all the way around the back because the place was so crowded when we got there. I kept handing Collin napkins and guided him toward the car, with his head tilted back.

As we neared the rear of the building, I got the uneasy feeling we were being watched.

It's just because there are no lights and it's dark, I kept telling myself.

The longer we walked and the closer to the car we got, the more unnerved I felt. It was almost as if my body was telling me to run, just get Collin to the car as fast as I could.

That's about the time I saw Paul walking briskly in our direction. I had to squint to see what it was, but even in the pale-yellow light of the security lamp attached to the club, I knew exactly what it was. The silver glint catching the light as his arms swung with his quickening gate in our direction.

Before I could even mutter a gasp, let alone a scream. Paul had raised the gun up, pointing it right at my face. We were not even twenty feet from the car, but there was no way we could make it there before Paul could pull the trigger.

"Whoa man!" Collin said, stepping forward, once again blocking me from Paul and forgetting all about his nose.

Paul shifted his aim at Collin now.

"Shut up fag, you'll get your turn!" Paul shouted in a voice so sinister, it chilled me to the bone.

"We can talk about this." Collin told him in his most reassuring tone. "No one needs to get hurt here."

"I SAID SHUT UP!" Paul shouted again. Pointing the gun rapidly back and forth from Collin to me.

"Get on your knees!" He added.

"Okay man. Whatever you want. Just let Eric leave." Collin pleaded as we both got down on our knees.

"No one is going anywhere!" Paul screamed. Cocking the hammer of his gun back.

That sound is something I will remember for as long as I live.

Click! Click!

It wasn't a loud noise, but it was most definitely a distinctive one.

My fear was overwhelming, my body started to vibrate. It felt like jolts of electricity were sparking from my head to my toes. My tongue was even tingling like when you stick it to a nine-volt battery, a metallic taste filled my mouth, every hair on my body was standing on end. It was as if I could feel the energy building up, flaring out wards to my fingertips.

Just then, Collin bolted to his feet and started toward Paul. It all seemed to happen so fast and all at once, yet somehow, it also seemed to be in slow motion.

I saw Collin moving toward Paul, but I was frozen, unable to move or speak. It was like watching some horrible movie.

I know I have bad luck, but this is ridiculous.

As Collin was just about to reach Paul and grapple for the gun, I saw the flash and heard the deafening boom. I screamed, but I'm not sure if I screamed out loud or only in my head?

Then the energy burst from my body, it felt as though it ripped me into pieces. My outstretched palms were set ablaze with a brilliant blue light.

Paul flew backwards, into the air, the energy pulsing from my hands seeming to shove him back. His huge muscled body, flinging away from us. He looked as though he were just a human sized rag doll flying through the air. It was as if some invisible truck just barreled over him, never slowing down. His body hit the ground with a bone shattering thud as he rolled several times before stopping where he laid.

I looked back to Collin, just as he fell to his knees, then he slumped over on his side with his back still turned to me. I was unable to move and all I could think was that I would give anything just for Collin to be okay. I would gladly give my own life to save his.

I looked back again, in the direction Paul had landed. His mangled body laying limp and unmoving, blood seeping from what seemed to be every part of him. Every limb was twisted and contorted in the most unnatural positions.

Was I really seeing this, was this some kind of dream?

Surely this couldn't be real, I had to be imagining the whole thing!

I focused back to Collin and used every bit of my being, to get the energy to stand.

What the hell just happened?

My ears were still ringing from the gun fire, my head was all cloudy and hazy, my vision blurred in and out of focus. I wobbled a bit to catch my balance and somehow managed to stagger over to where Collin was laying.

I think he was okay? I didn't see any blood, that was a good sign.

I flopped to the ground beside him, gravel dug into my knees and it stung as it cut into me. I kept calling his name, with no response, I started to shake him to get him to wake up.

He was still unmoving, I was screaming his name now. My voice was harsh and my throat was on fire, I felt like I had swallowed a box of nails and threw them back up.

RED!

There was a warm red liquid all over my hands.

Was it from me?
I didn't think I had been shot?

They do say that sometimes you don't feel any pain because of all the adrenaline.

I gave myself a quick once over, I didn't see any blood coming from me.

Oh god, this can't be happening.

I used what was left of my energy, rolled Collin over on his back, my eyes still trying to focus, but I saw the blood now.

Collin was shot!

There was so much blood, thick and red staining his shirt.

WHY!

Why is this happening? I kept thinking over and over.

I could see the hole left behind from the bullet, right below his left shoulder. He was still breathing, but only barely. I slumped over his lifeless body and started to cry uncontrollably.

I listened to his heartbeat, the rhythmic whomp whomp, whomp whomp, whomp... whomp...

Is his heart slowing down or am I about to pass out!?

Everything was starting to fade in and out around me and I heard sirens off in the distance. I could see the blue and red lights flashing, though, blurry through my teary eyes, I could see them getting closer.

I heard someone say, "Son, are you okay?"

A paramedic I assume? Maybe a police officer, I wasn't exactly sure.

I tried to make out a face, just as everything disappeared to blackness and I lost consciousness.

Chapter 9

Am I still alive or had I died?

The smell of cleaners and disinfectants stung my nose.

I must be alive, surely if I were dead, I wouldn't hurt so damn bad.

Every muscle in my body ached, like I was torn apart and put back together. I felt like I had been thrown off a cliff, only to be taken back to the top and flung off it once more, hitting every jagged rock and bump on the way down. At first I was miserable, but then relieved.

Pain is a good thing I suppose, at least with the pain, I know I am definitely still alive.

I tried to open my eyes, but they seemed to be glued shut. There was a blinding white light overhead.

I pried my eyes open, blinked a few times and look around the room, squinting from the blinding lights overhead. Obviously, I had been taken to a hospital.

The whirring of machines and the beeping of the EKG sounded like they were amplified to the max, it made me feel like my head was going to explode. I was lying in a single bed with the back propped up and colored wires were attached to my chest and head that led across the hospital bed to the machines and monitors. There was a very minimalist vibe to the room, no paintings or pictures hanging on the walls. Just a bright white floor, ceiling and walls. It was very sterile looking.

The only color in the whole room was the little blue flower and paisley pattern on the gown I had been placed in and the wires hooked to me.

Where is Collin? Was my first thought.

I suddenly felt frightened as I recalled turning Collin over and seeing all the blood. The hole left behind from where he had been shot, the top of his shoulder, was the wet and sticky, red fluid flowing from it.

The blood from his nose had nearly dried and was a darker shade of crimson. There was so much blood everywhere.

The panic flowed over me again as if it had just happened. I had to see him, make sure he was at least okay.

I threw the covers to the side and started ripping off the tubes and wires coming from what seemed to be every inch of me. The pain that was shooting all over my body, totally forgotten.

My only thought was getting to Collin, to be by his side like he always had been for me. After all he had come to my rescue and saved my life, only this time it was for real. I would probably be dead now if it weren't for Collin. I shook my head to clear my thoughts. I didn't have time to think about that now. I had to get to him somehow.

My head was pounding and the room started spinning. I felt like I was going to hurl. I leaned over the bed and tried to slowly breathe in and out, to keep me from falling over, I had to brace my hands on my knees.

Blood was starting to trickle down my arm from where I had ripped out the I.V. and the sight of my blood dripping down my arm started to make me queasy.

That was all I needed to send me over the edge, I started to vomit. The sensation of my stomach forcing up what little bit was left in there, caused my head to feel like it was seriously going to pop and I felt as though the veins in my neck would burst.

Just then a nurse came rushing in to stop me from getting out of bed. The monitors going ballistic with warning bells and beeps. I had hardly even noticed them in my haste to get out of the bed.

She grabbed my arms and restrained me. She was quite beautiful I noticed. Maybe in her late twenties or early thirties. Her auburn hair pulled tightly to the back in a simple yet elegant French twist, she had tired, kind eyes. Obviously, she worked long hours and wasn't affected by throw up.

"Let me go you bitch! I need to see Collin!" I screamed at her.

I shocked myself, that was totally out of character for me to be so rude, but I was too worried and too drowsy to care.

"If you don't calm down, I'll be forced to sedate you." She said in a surprisingly calm tone, as if she were used to being called a bitch.

I fought her for only a few seconds more, as I was so weak, I finally calmed myself and decided to stop struggling since I was obviously going to lose this battle and would rather lose it while awake than drugged and comatose. Not to mention, she was surprisingly strong for such a petite woman.

"I'm sorry" I pleaded. "Please! Where is Collin?"

"If you are referring to the gentleman that came in with you, he is in the I.C.U.." She said a with a little more brass.

I supposed she could see from the look of terror on my face that I was upset. I was already trying to choke back the tears.

She looked at me then sighed. "I'm not sure of his condition, but the last time I checked in on him he was stable. Not out of the woods yet, but stable." She reassured me with a little more tenderness.

"Thank you, again I'm sorry. I swear I am not normally like that." I said. Unable to look her in the eyes. "I'm just so worried about Collin and I need to see him, to make sure he is alright." I told her.

"Look, I'll tell you what, you can't see him now, but if you promise to be good and not rip out your IV's again. I'll keep you updated as soon as I hear anything else, deal?" She asked, now smiling at me.

I just nodded and smiled the best I could.

"My name is Rachel, if you need anything at all just press this button, I'm right down the hall." She pointed to the little red call button that was connected to my bed.

"Thank you so much!" I told her as she strode out of the room.

Chapter 10

As I laid there, I kept replaying the events over and over in my head. I didn't even know how long ago it happened?

How long was I in here, a few hours, a few days? Where were my parents, should I call them? Why hadn't I thought to ask Rachel before she left, how long I had been here.

I would feel horrible to call her in here just to ask her that, especially after the way I spoke to her. I would just have wait till she came back to check up on me again, then I'd ask her how long we had been here.

It didn't even seem real, everything that happened. I could see it so vividly now that it was done and over with. It was as though the images would be burned into my brain forever.

I remember seeing the brilliant blue light dancing down my arms like bolts of lightning and swirling around my fingertips like a Jacob's ladder and I recalled seeing it just as the shot rang out and the pop of the gun deafened me.

The light, bursting from my fingers like an explosion, heading straight for Paul, as it contacted his body, he recoiled and contorted as he flew through the air, the lightning like fibers flowing from my body to his, cutting him like tiny little razor blades, tearing at his flesh.

Was that real or did I imagine the whole thing? I wondered. They say stress does the weirdest things to the mind. Surely it wasn't real, was it? Oh my god!

I was going to drive myself crazy just thinking about it.

To distract myself, I turned on the TV and started flipping through the channels. I was blindly channel surfing, not even paying attention to what was on the station before I flipped to the next. I again found myself thinking of Collin. I was hoping so badly that he was going to be okay.

Why did he always have to be the hero? Better yet, why did I always have to be such a coward?

I turned off the TV, I wasn't going to be able to focus on anything even if I did find something half way interesting to watch.

The doctor came in to check on me, while looking over my chart he asked. "So, how are we feeling today?"

"Okay, I suppose. What's wrong with me and why am I still hooked to all this crap?" I retorted.

He looked at me nonchalantly. "When you came in here you were unconscious and dehydrated. The I.V. is to return fluids and the wires are to monitor your brain waves and heart rate. We are just crossing our T's and dotting our I's." He said. "And you had some irregularities in some of your tests that we did and we want to make sure everything is good before we release you."

"Oh, okay. So, what does that mean when you said I had irregularities in some of my tests?" I asked.

"It just means that some of the tests were inconclusive and that we need to monitor you for a while to make sure it is safe for you to go home." He reiterated. "The police are here and have a few questions for you, if you are up for it, I'll send them in?" He added.

Police?

What would the police want to talk to me about? I wondered, half way in a panic.

"Sure." Is all I managed to say.

The doctor turned to leave and shortly after he walked out, two officers came in to my room.

Damn it! I can't believe I didn't ask how Collin was doing!

He had caught me off guard when he said the police wanted to talk to me.

"Mr Summers, I'm Detective Humphrey and this is Detective Bishop. We have a few questions for you if you don't mind?" The older officer asked abrasively.

Flashing his badge in my direction.

He was a little more disheveled than the younger officer. His greying hair, wavy with tufts of curls going this way and that. He looked like he had just woken up and he had on an old leather jacket, white tee shirt and blue jeans. He reminded me of an older Elvis impersonator trying to relive his younger years or an old greaser from the 50's

If I don't mind he asks?

As if I had a choice either way?

I don't know why he even bothered with the politeness of asking if I mind, formalities I suppose.

"Um, sure." I said trying not to sound guilty.

Guilty? What did I have to feel guilty about?

I really didn't know what happened and if what I thought happened, really happened the way it happened....

Wow!

Maybe I am going crazy?

I'm even starting to confuse myself in my own head. I can't tell them what I think happened because they will for sure think I'm crazy and would lock me up in the closest nuthouse and throw away the key. I took in a deep breath and cleared my thoughts as I tried to put on a smile.

"Eric, may I call you Eric?" The younger officer said politely.

He had a much softer tone to his voice and unlike his partner, was dressed in uniform. He seemed to be a lot more professional looking with his freshly pressed uniform. He was obviously new at the job, but you could tell he had a lot more pride in his appearance than his older counterpart. He had light brown hair with golden brown highlights. I couldn't tell if he had it colored or if it was naturally highlighted, from the sun maybe? His eyes were the same color brown as mine, but warmer, with flecks of gold. He was tall and muscular and very attractive I noticed.

He must be the good cop I thought to myself, trying to hold back a giggle.

"Sure." I smiled. Then winced from the pain.

He obviously didn't notice because he continued anyway.

"Can you tell us, in your own words what happened last night?" He asked then touched his pen to the pad he was holding to take notes.

Okay, last night is what he said. So now, I at least had a time line of how long I had been here.

I looked out the window at the dark sky, close to twenty-four hours, that's how long Collin has been in the I.C.U.

I had to get to him or at least know if he was okay. I blinked a few times to clear the new tears starting to form in my eyes again.

"Well…" I said. Then paused. "I really don't know? Everything happened so fast and I got light headed and passed out. I really am confused as to what happened." I stammered.

At least it was only half a lie. I really didn't know for sure what had happened.

"It's okay." He said. "Maybe now isn't a good time? If you can think of anything, anything at all, feel free to call me at this number."

He handed me his card. Detective Riley Bishop, Precinct 9, and a phone number, it was a basic card, but I guess it got the job done.

"Thank you, Detective Bishop, I will. Sorry I couldn't be any more help." I told him.

"It's fine. It will come back to you. Just get some rest and call me if you have any new information." He nodded to the card he had just handed me as he turned to leave.

"Detective Bishop. What happened to the other guy? Paul, he is the one that shot my friend. Is he okay?" I asked grudgingly.

Detective Bishop turned back to me and said. "He didn't make it. Looks like you boys were lucky this time. Someone must have seen that he had a gun and ran him over. All the evidence points to a hit and run. I guess he was mangled pretty badly and the suspect got scared and took off! Don't worry, we will find whomever did this."

"Thanks." Is all I could say as I watched them leave my room.

Hit and run? Did I hear him correctly? I may have been a little disoriented, but I am pretty damn sure I would have seen a vehicle mowing Paul over? Maybe I did just imagine the whole thing? He did say all the evidence pointed to a hit and run.

I still had to find out if Collin was okay, any news was better than no news at all. I had to know something soon.

Should I call the nurses station?

She did say that she would let me know as soon as she knew anything. The suspense of waiting was killing me though.

I started thinking of Collin again, lying in that room all by himself and started to cry.

Why am I such a baby? I thought, but I couldn't help it. The tears flowed endlessly until I cried myself to sleep.

Chapter 11

I woke up the next morning, the light from the morning sun blinding me through the open window, but not as harsh as the fluorescent lights during the night.

I wasn't hooked to all the machines and I.V.'s like last night and my pain was more bearable now, still there, but bearable.

How had I not woke up when they came to detach them? I must have really been out of it.

My throat was so dry and scratchy and I needed something to drink so badly. I reached for the small table to the right of my bed and grabbed for the cup.

Shit!

It was empty! Of course, I don't know why I expected anything else.

I sighed heavily and reached to the other side to get to the call button, I pressed it and waited.

A voice came over the intercom.

"Yes? Can I help you?" Rachel asked.

"Yes ma'am, may I have some water please?" I said, my voice cracking as I spoke.

"Of course, I'll be in momentarily." She replied.

I had to pee so bad that my bladder might burst. I figured that I could make it to the bathroom and back before she could make it in here.

I swung my legs over the bed and waited till the room stopped spinning. I placed my feet on the cold white tile and made my way to the bathroom, shuffling slowly with each step.

When I came out of the bathroom, Rachel was already in my room with a pitcher of water and a cup with a bendy straw. I was so thirsty I could hardly form the words to speak, but forgot all about my thirst the second I saw her.

"How is Collin!" I tried to shout, but it came out more as a harsh whisper.

"Water first, then we can talk." She said with a smile.

I didn't want the stupid water now!

Why couldn't she just tell me? I thought angrily, but wasn't going to be rude to her again.

I rushed back over to the bed and sat down, guzzling nearly the whole cup in a few swallows. It hurt so bad, yet was so satisfying, until I started choking, spitting water all down the front of me and on to the floor.

"Easy now." Rachel said chuckling. "Slow down, there's more where that came from."

"Okay, I drank some. Now can you please tell me if Collin is okay?" I pleaded, wiping the water off my face with my hand.

She sat on the side of the bed next to me and placed her hand on my shoulder. Her eyes looking into mine with such tenderness. The suspense was killing me and the way she was acting I already knew what she was going to say! My vision began to haze over with the tears forming once again. My face began to burn and I could physically feel the blood leaving. I felt like I was going to be sick again, I started to hyperventilate.

"Please tell me it isn't true; please tell me it isn't true." I repeated over and over while rocking back and forth, trying not to vomit.

"Calm down sweetheart." She said. Worry now crossing her face. "Collin is fine."

"What?!" I exclaimed. I wasn't sure if I had heard her correctly.

"Collin is okay!" She repeated. "He got out of surgery this morning. I was actually already headed down to tell you when you buzzed the nurses station."

I started to laugh uncontrollably. The happiness I felt was indescribable. I hugged Rachel till my arms hurt. She pried my arms loose and giggled.

"See, everything was just fine. The bullet entered through his clavicle, shattering the bone and imbedded in his scapula, but the doctors removed it and patched him up. He will be in a lot of pain for a while and the healing will be slow, but he will be fine, and you want to know what else?" She asked. Not giving me time to answer. "You were the first thing he asked about when he woke up and he wants to see you. Would you like me to take you to him?" She asked.

"Of course!" I shouted. I couldn't even pretend to hold in my excitement.

"Okay then, I'll go and get you a wheelchair." She said. Smiling as she left the room.

Rachel returned a short while later. She must have already had a chair waiting for me.

I almost fell into the wheelchair as Rachel pushed it to the side of my bed. Collin was doing okay and I was finally going to get to see him.

She wheeled me down the hallway to the elevators where I impatiently waited for the doors to open and she pushed me in the open door and pressed the button for level four. The elevator came to a stop on the fourth floor and the doors opened.

My heart was racing and my stomach was fluttering with butterflies. We came to a stop at room 407 and Rachel rolled me through the doorway.

Collin was laying on his back still connected to the same colorful wires and clear tubes I had been hooked to only hours before. His eyes were closed and he looked so delicate and vulnerable just lying there in that hospital bed. I wheeled myself over to the side of his bed and took his hand.

He opened his eyes and smiled.

"Hey there! Took you long enough and look, we're twinkies!" He said pointing to our hospital gowns.

Collin always had to joke. Even in the most serious of situations.

"I am so sorry Collin!" I exclaimed "It's all my fault!"

"Shhh. It's no one's fault. I'm just glad we are both okay." He squeezed my hand reassuringly.

I began to cry, only this time from happiness. I was unable to speak from the excitement I felt.

I just laid my head down on his hand and listened to the EKG beep to the rhythm of his heartbeat, a sound that, only hours ago, was the bane of my existence, was now my saving grace.

I just sat there and listened to the low toned beeping and Collin rested his other hand on my head. He was going to be okay and I was going to make sure of that. I closed my eyes and concentrated back on the sounds of the EKG and smiled to myself.

Beep....beep.... beep.... beep....

Chapter 12

The hospital called our parents and they rushed down and made it to the hospital before I was released. My mom was frantic, it took me and my dad both to calm her down. At one point, I even thought Rachel was going to have to come and sedate her.

It took all I had just to convince her that I really was okay and that Collin would be fine. She was insistent on the fact that she warned me it would be a bad idea to leave so far from home. It was almost impossible to tell her that it was just a freak accident and that I wasn't really that far from home anyway.

I love my mom to death, but she hovered over me like a protective mother hen all week. I was surprised she even let me go to the bathroom by myself. However, it was kind of nice to not have to stay in the apartment all by myself.

Collin and I, all but begged the hospital to let me just stay there, but that was out of the question. At least Rachel let me sneak in his room early and stay a little past visiting hours. I really was starting to like her.

The night nurse, Beatrice, on the other hand, was a total bitch, not that I told her that, but she was definitely a stickler for the rules.

My mother, aside from being overly protective, took me shopping and got us needed supplies for the apartment. I told her that she didn't have to do that, but I also know that it made her feel good to do it, so I just went along with it. It could feel a little smothering with her at times, but I know that she only did these things because she loved me.

She decided that she was going to stay in the apartment with me until Collin came home, my dad tried to talk her into staying at the hotel, but I guess he decided it was going to be a losing battle and finally unloaded their suitcases from the car.

Collin's parents needed no convincing, they wouldn't dare stay at the apartment away from room service and all the amenities of fine dining and shopping.

Not that I am complaining, I was grateful that they kept their distance. My mother was enough to deal with as is.

It's been more than a week now and things are finally starting to get back to normal. Our parents decided that they would only stay until Collin was released and then they would head back home. They have been driving me nuts with all the worrying. They even tried to talk Collin and me in to moving back home and going to a community college closer to home. It took a lot of persuasion from both Collin and myself to assure them that we would be okay and that the whole ordeal at the bar really was just a freak accident.

My parents were even harder to convince, but after hours of talking and debating, I think I finally got them to ease off, for a little while at least. My mother just sighs and sits in silence. She always goes right for the guilt trip. She has that down pat.

Collin's mom and dad were a lot easier to convince. They are good at just sweeping things under the rug and calling it a day. I am sure they are genuinely concerned for both of us, but they just show it a little differently.

Chapter 13

My excitement is in overdrive today because Collin gets to come home tomorrow. He has already missed a full week of school, but our parents and I had a meeting together with the school board and they decided to let him make up his lost hours over the weekends and with extra work, because of the devastating ordeal that took place.

College was really the last thing on my mind here recently. Although, I still had to keep up the pretenses for our parent's sake or they really would have made us come home with them.

It was as if the school didn't want to know what really happened either. They kept calling it a travesty.

A travesty! What the hell was that supposed to mean?

The definition of a travesty is a false, absurd, or distorted representation of something. I for one, took that offensively, but kept my mouth shut, which within itself is a miracle. I sometimes find it difficult to keep my mouth shut and bite my tongue in certain situations. I decided that this was one of those times that I should.

Besides, we said nothing that was false, but I suppose that didn't really matter to the school. It honestly wouldn't surprise me in the least if Collin's parents threw some money at the college to build a new science wing or something, just so they would let Collin catch up.

I of course have been taking Collin his homework and helping him study while he was still in the hospital, so he really won't be that far behind. Besides, the hospital let me stay with him longer than normal visiting hours, on one condition, that we were studying. Mostly we just talked and goofed around or watched some TV though, but at least he would not be that far behind and he has always done really well in school.

Nurse Beatrice or Nurse Biatch, as Collin and I had affectionately come to know her, was working tonight and of course she made me leave right on time. It was almost like she was waiting by Collin's door, watching the clock. I really did dislike that woman!

It was okay though, in just a few short hours I would be able to take him home. However, I was certain that the night would last forever!

I woke up early after a sleepless night, to get ready to get Collin from the hospital. Both our parents are staying until tonight to make sure Collin gets settled in. We make our way to the hospital and they already have him down and ready for release. I think that he is just as ready to be home as much as I am to have him home.

As soon as we pull up to the patient drop off/pick up lane, his eyes light up with excitement and I practically flung myself from the moving vehicle before it even came to a complete stop. I ran up to him as fast as I could and gave him a big bear hug.

"Ouch! Careful now. I am injured you know." Collin laughed.

"Sorry, I forgot what a delicate flower you are." I teased as we both burst into laughter.

We acted as though we hadn't seen each other in weeks, but I was just here last night.

We spent the whole day before planning what we were going to do as soon as he got out. Collin was making jokes about going to Club 23 to come up with a few new dance moves.

I normally think he is funny, but when it comes to this matter, he thinks he is a lot funnier than he actually is, but I think that's just his way of coping with the whole situation. He tends to take things that are very serious and makes them into a joke.

In reality, I am sure he is still scared and the last thing he will do for a while is go to the club.

I myself, am scared shitless. I still wake up in the middle of the night drenched in sweat and screaming. It is a life altering situation when you are inches from death and have a gun pointed straight at your head.

I can't even start to imagine how Collin feels, he was actually shot on top of everything else.

I would probably be in the nut house for sure if I had been the one that was shot, but I would have gladly taken his place. I guess we never really know what we will do until we are put in that situation.

We got Collin situated at our apartment and say our goodbyes to our parents after dinner. I couldn't wait for them to leave for the better part of the week, but now that they were driving away, it was a little sad.

I appreciate everything that they do and I may sometimes seem a little ungrateful, but I really mean it when I say I will miss them. My mother, of course, took leaving the hardest. I thought we were going to have to rent a bigger apartment with a third bedroom for her to stay.

Collin has a pretty long recovery time ahead of him. The doctor said it could be three to six months or even more. I feel bad for him, but also plan to make his healing process as smooth as possible. He is still in a lot of pain, but tries to play the tough guy.

I don't buy it, plus I know all his tricks. I guess the fact that the hospital put him on some pretty intense painkillers sure doesn't hurt the matter either.

The bullet went through his left shoulder and unfortunately, he is left handed, but I plan to be his 'left hand man'. Out of guilt that he was the one that got shot, I pretended I could only use my left hand for a couple days, because I am right handed, but I had no difficulties with it. Not that I would dare tell Collin that.

Like I said, he tries to play the tough guy, but he can be a big baby too. I guess I really don't mind, after all, he did save my life.

Had Collin not been there or tried to grapple for the gun, then I could have been the one in the hospital for over a week or even worse, in the morgue. Who's to say that Paul wouldn't have just killed us both for no reason. Insane people rarely need motive, and Paul was clearly insane.

Collin doesn't really remember anything from that night either. That's what he told the police anyway.

He said that after the gun discharged, he can't remember anything after that, he says he never saw Paul flying through the air or hit by a vehicle, just nothing.

I guess that's a good thing, it corroborated everything I had said as well.

However, I think the police started to get a little frustrated with us, not that we could help it. I don't think Collin really did remember anything and I still wasn't sure that I did either.

Not that I would say aloud what I thought happened, to anyone other than Collin.

"So, how are you feeling?" I asked Collin as we were preparing for bed.

"I'm okay I guess, better now that I am home." He replied.

"I'm really glad to have you back, but can we talk?" I asked him, unable to look him in the eyes.

"Sure." He said looking concerned. "What's wrong?"

I started to speak then stopped. I didn't know if I could tell him what was on my mind without bawling like a baby again.

"Come on Eric, tell me what's the matter. You can always talk to me and tell me anything." He said with a pitiful tone.

I could never refuse him when he looked at me with that pouty face and puppy dog eyes.

"Well," I started. "I don't really know where to even begin? I just wanted to say that I am sorry again and that I am so grateful that you are my friend." I told him.

"Oh my god! Shut up!" He laughed. "I thought you were going to tell me something serious?"

"I am serious!" I retorted.

"Hey, you are my best friend and I will always love you no matter what. I want you to always remember that and we will always be friends, just as I will always be there for you." He said. "And besides, you have nothing to be sorry for. Nothing would have kept me from protecting you. Ever!"

"I feel the same about you!" I exclaimed. "But I just hate that you got hurt and I feel that it was all my fault!"

"Come here." He whispered, pulling me to him with his good arm.

I just leaned over and we hugged for what seemed to be forever.

"Come lay with me, I don't really want to be alone right now." He said.

"Okay." I said, still pouting.

I crawled under the covers with him and put my head on his chest. I was careful not to put my arm over his hurt shoulder and I was lullabied once more by the rhythm of his heart. Only this time instead of fear and panic, it was in complete comfort. I breathed in heavily and took in the scent of his cologne. It was my favorite, the one I got him last year for Christmas.

I watched out the open window at the stars in the sky till my eyelids felt like they weighed a ton and I could no longer keep them open. We laid there in silence until we both drifted to sleep. For the first time in over a week, I finally had a dreamless sleep.

Chapter 14

The next morning, I woke again to the smell of bacon and eggs cooking. For a second, I forgot all about the past couple weeks and woke with a smile.

I stretched for a long while and sat up on the edge of the bed just about the time I heard pans clatter to the floor.

"DAMN IT! What the hell!" Collin yelled from the kitchen.

I ran down the hall to see what had happened.

"Are you okay?" I asked, before I had even made it around the corner.

"I can't do a damn thing with this stupid sling on!" He growled.

I couldn't help, but chuckle at him.

Collin was always a morning person and I was supposed to be the grumpy one.

"Here, let me help you." I said. Still laughing a little.

Collin just gave me the evil eye and stepped to the side.

"You go sit down and I'll make you breakfast for once." I said.

"I was hoping to have it made before you woke up. I thought that I could at least do that." He said with such melancholy.

I laughed out loud this time.

"You are so pitiful, it's cute." I told him.

Then he gave me the worst dirty look and burst into laughter himself.

It was a welcoming sight to see him actually laugh. A for real laugh, not his usual, let's let everyone think everything is perfectly fine, laugh. He thinks that he has me fooled, but I know him all too well and he wasn't fooling me.

Today was the first time he had laughed since the night at the club. I was afraid that I would never get to see those little dimples on his cheeks again.

We chatted over breakfast and it was as if nothing ever happened.

I wanted to talk about what went on at the club that night, but every time I thought to bring it up I stopped myself. Why would I try to ruin the mood by bringing it up again?

I had tried to ask him about it a few times at the hospital, but Collin would just change the subject or divert his attention to something else and act as though he didn't hear me, or he would just look down and say that he didn't want to talk about that right now.

Then he would get all depressed and sulk the rest of the day. I didn't want to do that to him all over again, I would just wait for the right time, before I tried to ask him about it.

Chapter 15

Now it's Monday and we are off to school. Something that I had looked so forward to before and now it was torture. We had to sit through the mundane lectures and learn all the basic crap that I couldn't have cared less about.

At least the last class was a little better. We got to dance and learn new routines. Our instructor was pretty cool too, she was quite a bit older, but at least she was entertaining.

Collin and I had decided that we would walk to school, since it was only a few short blocks. I enjoyed the walks to and from anyway. We could talk about our day and the new people we had met and about which professors we did or didn't like, but Collin was acting a little down today and we walked home in silence.

As soon as we walked in the door he turned to me and asked if we could talk.

"Of course," I said. Walking to the table to sit down. "What's the matter?"

"I told the police that I didn't remember anything from that night, but that's not completely true." Collin told me.

"What do you mean?" I asked, a little concerned now.

"I saw what you did. I can't explain it, but I did see something." He said.

"What are you talking about? What did you see?" I asked incredulously.

"I don't really know for sure, but I know I saw something." He continued. "I saw your hands light up like a plasma globe. Then that Paul guy got hit like he was struck by lightning. I know that it sounds crazy, but I know you did something to him. I don't know how, but it was you that saved us."

I just sat in silence and looked at him dumbfounded. My stomach was rolling and I felt as if I might vomit and my brain was racing a hundred miles per hour.

What was I going to tell him? Should I tell him what I thought happened or should I lie and pretend I don't know what he is talking about?

"I think maybe you were just seeing things. I didn't do anything and besides, the police said that it was a hit and run!" I exclaimed a little too excitedly.

"Just stop!" Collin scolded. "I know I'm not crazy or just imagining things. I have been reliving that night since it happened!" He almost yelled. His tone with me took me by surprise.

He never talked to me like that. I felt like my throat was going to swell shut. I didn't know if I could even keep this up anymore.

"I'm sorry Collin. I really don't know what happened. I was so scared that he was going to hurt you and I just reacted. I had no control over it." I blurted out.

Tears started to form and roll down my cheeks. I was kind of glad that he had seen it too. I was so afraid that it was me that was the crazy one or that I had just made the whole thing up in my head.

It made me feel so much better to finally have it out in the open, to be able to talk about it and maybe come up with an explanation together. I was also afraid that he would think that I was some kind of freak or he'd be afraid of me.

What if he turned me in to the police for killing Paul? My mind was racing with question after question.

"Can you do it again?" He finally asked with a little more excitement than I was expecting, pulling me back to the real world.

"Do what?" I recoiled. "I am not even sure how I did it the first time."

"Come on Eric. Just try it." He antagonized.

"How!?" I argued.

"Well, I don't know?" He urged. "Just try anything, concentrate."

"Okay!" I said. "I will try, but I don't think it will work."

I sighed and closed my eyes while trying to concentrate on my hands, as I sat there for a moment trying to force the energy to flow through me again.

I opened one eye to look at Collin and he had the most intense look on his face. I couldn't help it. I burst into uncontrollable laughter.

"What?" He jumped back as if he was startled. "What happened?"

"You look constipated!" I said, hardly able to contain my laughter.

"Whatever! Shut up!" He exclaimed. Then he too started laughing.

"This is dumb." I told him, still giggling. "I won't deny that something did happen that night, but I really don't think it was me? Or at least not something I can control."

"You're right." He agreed. "Hell, maybe we both just imagine the whole thing?"

"Probably so." I concurred. "Let's just forget the electric fingers for tonight and say that we did just imagine the whole thing. It's too weird anyway and they say stress can do all kinds of things to the mind."

"You got a deal. It does all sound a little too crazy." He said.

"Good." I said in compliance. "Would you like a snack?" I asked.

"Yes! I'm starving." He said smiling.

I got up and made my way to the kitchen to make us a sandwich and sweet tea, then sat down at the table with Collin to eat and start studying.

He already had his books out and was intently reading through a few pages when I came to sit across the round table from him.

"You think you can help me with my History homework?" He asked.

"Sure. Pass me your book and I will start reading." I said, pointing to his History book, just as it slid across the table to rest directly in front of me, seemingly all by itself.

"Um! You saw that, right?!" I said with dubiety.

"I sure as hell did! Now that's badass!" He blurted with elation.

Chapter 16

Walking down the long corridor of the college, I was daydreaming about all the possibilities.

What did all this mean? Was I some kind of mutant or was I destined to be a great superhero? Even a better question, how had this happened and why was it happening to me? Nothing good ever happened to me, aside from Collin. I had always had such shitty luck my whole life and then suddenly, I seemed to be handed a gift.

I had no idea how it worked or how I did some of the things that I have done.

I would sit and concentrate until I thought my head was going to explode and yet nothing ever happened. I had tried to move several objects with my mind and couldn't even get a piece of paper to move. I really didn't know how I was able to move an entire human, or even worse, how had I killed him?

After Collin and I realized that it was me that had killed Paul, I kind of went into a deep depression for a while. It is a hard thing to deal with, knowing that you took another humans life. I tried to justify it by telling myself that it was self-defense and he was going to kill us both if I hadn't done anything, but that didn't really help the matter a whole lot.

Collin seems to be okay with everything. I think he wishes he had some kind of ability as well. He keeps trying to reassure me that there was nothing I could have done and that it wasn't my fault. I suppose he is right though?

It's not like I had meant to do it, but that only helps slightly. I do sleep a little better now though, but sometimes I still wake in a cold sweat and jolt up with a scream starting to build up in my throat before I realize where I am. I keep having nightmares about killing Paul, but sometimes instead of Paul it is someone else. One night it was Collin, that was the worst feeling ever. Other nights it's another friend or family member and sometimes it is even a complete stranger. I still wake up terrified.

Had I really meant to kill him? Would I kill someone else? Should I turn myself in?

These are just a few of the questions that ran constantly through my mind. What kind of person could do such a thing? Something that started off to be a gift, something that was so 'cool' was turning in to a nightmare. Quite literally and figuratively. What kind of person was I and shouldn't I feel worse?

"Hey Eric. Wait up?" I heard a voice coming from behind me.

It was Clair. Clair was in our preforming arts class. She was pretty cool. She had been nice to me from day one so we pretty much hit it off from the start.

Clair was also a big help to me while Collin was in the hospital and she gave me an excuse to get away from my parents from time to time. She was a tiny thing, maybe 110 pounds soaking wet, but she was pretty too. Clair had the nerdy vibe to her, but you could tell if she put a little effort in her appearance she would be quite beautiful.

She has blonde hair with blue eyes that popped because of her excessively long lashes and her porcelain skin was flawless.

She has more of what I would call an emo or goth like kind of style, with the dark clothes and dark makeup. Although, she had a wide range of styles from wearing all black to her rainbow-colored socks.

"Oh, hey Clair. How's it going?" I asked her as she jogged to catch up to me.

"Pretty good." She replied. "I was just going to see if you and Collin wanted to get together after class and work on our new dance routine or maybe go catch a movie? You seem really down lately and look like you could use a break?"

"I don't know Clair, I'm not really feeling it today." I sighed.

"Come on! It'll do ya some good to get out for a while!" She smirked. "Besides, I need an excuse to wear the new outfit I just bought!" She added excitedly.

"Okay." I laughed "Who could say no to that? Only because it's for your benefit though."

She giggled and let out a little squeal of delight. "Awesome! I'll meet up with y'all after last period." She said as she strode off to her next class.

I made it to my class and sat down at my usual chair as the professor began his lecture. I couldn't even pay attention to what he was saying, I was so out of it today. I had no idea how I was going to make it through this year with a passing grade.

Thank god for books and test.

I have always tested well, even if I didn't know the material. Finally, my last class of the day. I loved this class, I could be myself and vent my stresses away through dancing.

Dancing was always so therapeutic to me, which is why I want to become an instructor at my own studio someday. Collin and Clair always beat me there and they were already chatting and stretching in our little corner of the studio.

"Hey guys." I forced a smile and waved at them.

"Hey Eric. How was your day?" Collin asked, smiling back.

"Mine was good." I lied.

Collin just looked at me with his look, the one that told me he knew that I was lying. He knew me all too well and I could never lie to him.

That's probably about the only thing that I don't like about Collin, is that I can never lie to him. He just smiled and nodded trying not to give me away to Clair, but I knew that I would be interrogated as soon as we got home.

"Hello Eric." Clair waved. "Collin said he is down for a movie too so it's a threesome tonight." She joked.

Collin and I just laughed. It was a little weird to me to see a girl that was so crude. I think she had more of a potty mouth than even I did.

"You're so nasty." I told her as she shrugged her shoulders.

Clair could turn anything into a sexual or dirty situation. I think that's what I liked about her so much. She was more like one of the boys. I felt like I could be myself around her too. Our friendship was nothing like Collin and I had, but she was a good friend.

After class, we decided to walk Clair to her room to get changed and wait for her, then we would all three ride to the theatre together. I was glad, at least that way I had a little more time before Collin could give me the third degree.

We got to her dorm room and sat on the bed while Clair changed in the bathroom. I avoided eye contact with Collin, too afraid he would ask me what was really bothering me, so I just looked around her room.

Her room was one of the few that had a private bathroom and it was decorated in an eclectic manor. If a stranger were to walk in by accident, they probably wouldn't be able to tell if they had come into a boys or a girl's room. She has everything from pink princess stuff to camouflage.

"So? What do y'all think?" Clair asked as she came out of the bathroom and did a model walk and spun around.

She wore a dress that was floor length and dark midnight blue, but it had shimmers of silver and gold that sparkled throughout. Clair looked like an evening sky with stars that flickered as she spun.

"Beautiful!" Collin said then did a cat call.

"Wow, you look amazing." I told her truthfully. "But you do realize we are just going to a movie and not a five-star restaurant, right?" I added.

Clair giggled with delight.

"You guys! Stop it." She said, pretending to be shy.

"Now I feel underdressed." Collin teased her. Making her smile even more.

We rode to the theater, as Collin drove and Clair acted as DJ. They were laughing and singing along to the music as I just sat in the back seat and was happy that we were going to a movie so I had a little more time before Collin and I were left alone so he could interrogate me. He still doesn't understand why I am taking it out on myself so badly. He has told me repeatedly that it was self-defense and reminds me that the police think it was a hit and run and they are looking for a suspect that was driving a vehicle. I know that it was just self-defense, but it doesn't seem to help that much.

I try to keep telling myself that the way it happened doesn't change anything, that if I was able to get the gun, I don't think that the outcome would have changed any.

I would have done anything and everything I could to save Collin no matter what was used. Never mind the fact that it just happened to be some magic power or whatever the hell it was. I wish I knew how I had done it. I think that if I at least knew how, it would make me feel a little better.

The fact that I was bothered more that I didn't know how to control whatever it was that I did, bothered me more than the fact that I had taken another person's life with only using my mind.

Chapter 17

After the movie, we dropped Clair off at her dorm and headed back to the apartment. It was a short drive and Collin was driving very slowly. He drove the car to our designated parking spot and shifted it into park.

"Are you really okay?" He finally asked me.

"Yes, I'm fine. I am just a little stressed out." I reassured him.

He took my hand and smiled at me. This instantly made me feel better, just as it always did.

"You know you can tell me anything, right?" He asked.

"Of course I do." I said. "It's just that there isn't really anything to tell. I am just a little sad, but I'm fine, I promise." I added

"Okay, I just want you to be happy." He told me smiling.

"Come on, let's go in and you can come stay in my room tonight." He said as he got out of the car.

I loved staying in Collin's room. It felt so much more comfortable than in my own bed. I waited for Collin to get out of the bathroom and went in to brush my teeth while he got undressed. I took off my clothes, down to my underwear and headed over to Collin's room, he was already laying under the covers, so I turned out the lights and crawled under with him.

"Can I ask you something and if it makes you uncomfortable you can tell me?" He asked.

"Sure, I told you before that you can ask me anything Collin and we have been friends long enough that I highly doubt you could make me feel uncomfortable." I assured him.

"I usually don't sleep with anything on at night and I only have been when you sleep in here. Would it bother you if I didn't?" He asked, seemingly a little embarrassed

His shyness took me by surprise, Collin never got embarrassed about anything, especially nudity.

"Didn't what?" I asked, even though I knew exactly what he was talking about.

"Would it bother you if I took off my underwear and slept nude?" He reiterated. "If it's too weird, I won't do it." He added uncomfortably.

A lump formed again in my throat and butterflies fluttered in my tummy. Okay, maybe I was wrong.

I guess he could make me feel uncomfortable still, but not uncomfortable in a bad way, I was stunned.

I didn't even know really what to say. My worries were wiped away and now all I could think of was his naked body lying next to me all night.

"Um, sure. I don't care, if that's how you like to sleep." I stammered.

"Okay good. Only if you're sure it won't be too weird or creep you out?" He said, returning to his usual banter.

"Of course, not. Why would it bother me?" I laughed uneasily.

"Okay then. I'm glad you say that because I hate sleeping with underwear on. It is so constricting." He said as he pulled them off and flung them to the floor.

I just laid there, too afraid to move. I didn't really know how I felt about it. I suppose it really didn't bother me as much as I thought, but it was so confusing.

It was as though my own body was betraying me. I have always thought Collin was attractive, but never thought of him in a romantic way, not really.

Now with him laying only inches away from me, his naked body almost touching mine, my nerves were overloaded and I had goosebumps all over every inch of me. I could feel his body heat from under the covers, warming me and sending my blood rushing to my face. I felt like I was on fire and I began to tremble. He rolled over on his side and put his arm across my chest. His breath tickling my ear as he slowly breathed in and exhaled.

"Are you alright?" He asked sounding concerned.

"Yes! Why do you ask?" I said, startled by the sound of his voice.

"You're trembling and your heart is racing." He replied.

"I'm sorry!" I said. "I don't know why!"

I hadn't even realized I was shaking. He paused for a short while then I felt the weight of his body as he rolled over on top of me and he had his lips almost touching mine. I began to shake even more and I felt his hard on throbbing against me. My mind was in a whirlwind of haze, I felt the urge to push him away, yet I wanted him closer. I was torn between the two conflicting sides. I felt so stupid to just lay there like a lump on a log. My erection was pounding and it was twisted in the most uncomfortable position.

Now all I could think about was trying to reach down and adjust myself without Collin noticing what I was doing. I shifted slightly and made the proper adjustment. Our eyes met one another's gaze in the dim light of the nightlight in the hallway.

I could no longer contain my animalistic urge to ravish him so I leaned my head up toward his and closed my eyes. Then paused and waited, he too was unmoving.

Oh my god! I thought to myself. What if I was misreading him or what if he was just playing around or what if he had no sexual intentions toward me and I just opened myself up, invited him to come in to kiss me?

I felt so stupid now, how was I going to play this one off?

Chapter 18

That's about the time I felt his fingers glide through my hair as he gently grabbed a handful and pulled my head back while his other hand caressed my face. I felt his hot breath as it brushed against my cheek.

He was breathing so heavily, I thought he might hyperventilate, or was that me? It was too hard to tell at that point. The suspense of waiting was killing me.

What was he waiting for? Just kiss me damn it, take me now!

I was his slave, there for him to use and abuse any way he saw fit, I was his and that was the only thing that mattered in that moment.

That thought alone brought a smile to my face, the thought of being his, I was at the mercy of his will. I couldn't take it any longer, so I let out a soft whimper, begging him, pleading with him to take me and make me his.

I was breathing so heavily and my heart felt as though it would pound right out of my chest. He brushed his lips ever so gently against mine, softly at first then with more vigor. I let out a satisfying moan and he must have taken that as an invitation because he began to massage my tongue with his.

My mind was racing, yet I couldn't think. I shivered again as he slowly kissed down my cheek to my ear, then he nibbled softly on my earlobe before he made his way back to my lips.

I felt his hand as he slid it slowly down my body to the band of my underwear, gliding his fingers across my stomach, it made my body twitch and convulse as he silently pulled my underwear down and removed them the rest of the way with his feet. I felt the urge to stop him, but I wanted to feel our bodies touching skin to skin.

He pressed his body against mine, our sweat merging as I pulled Collin in closer to me. Even though we were about as close as two people could possibly be, I wanted him closer, no I wanted him inside me, in every way possible.

The urge to pull him into me almost unbearable, I let out another soft whimper, my back arched and my toes curled as I clenched my fingers, digging them into Collin's back.

I was afraid I had done it too hard at first, but he seemed to like it, he let out a groan of pleasure as he pressed his back deeper into my fingertips.

I was still silently begging and pleading with him to take me. I didn't understand what was going on. This was totally out of character for me, but oh well, who gave a damn? His body felt so amazing against mine and I never wanted the pleasurable torture to end.

The sensation of his scruff tickling my face as he moved from my ear once more and nibbled on my lower lip sent chills down my spine.

I slowly moved my hands up and down his body, sliding them up his chiseled abs, softly grazing his stomach with the back of my nails, then I made my way to his shoulders and I liked the way it made him quiver and arch his back, pressing his pelvis deeper into mine.

Then I made my way down to his pelvis and then wrapped my arms around his waist and ran my fingers up from the small of his back to his muscled shoulders.

My eyes were closed and I was memorizing his body, learning where every curve and muscle was and how he felt under my hands.

His smooth skin felt like velvet as his muscles twitched and he undulated under my soft touches, I pulled him closer to me once more, kissing his neck as he too let out a soft moan.

I could see in the dim light that his eyes were closed and he really did look like a Greek god, the sweat beads slowly forming, gliding down his body, I was in total ecstasy. It was hard to discern if this was real or if I was just having a lucid dream, but if I were dreaming, then I wasn't completely sure that I wanted to wake up.

Collin shifted his weight, making me spread my legs further as he slithered down my body, kissing every inch of me on his way down.

He paused at my belly button and looked up at me, his blonde hair was draped across one of his eyes and his hair was starting to stick together from the sweat.

I knew that his eyes were blue, but I never knew they were that blue. They seemed to be the color of a sapphire, but even more beautiful.

He smiled his crooked little smile, it was always my favorite smile and he knew it too. He always used it against me whenever he wanted to get his way.

All I could do is smile back at him, his sultry gaze had me transfixed, lost in our own little world and it was as if we were the only two people on the planet.

He resumed kissing me, starting with my hip, I grit my teeth and clawed at the sheets, doing my very best not to scream out loud. Slowly he ran his tongue across my stomach to give the other hip equal attention, all while his chin grazed the tip of my penis, which almost sent me over the edge.

I had never been with anyone sexually before. Well, no one other than myself of course and neither had Collin, but where had he learned to do these things? I guess he really was a natural at pretty much everything he did and no amount of practicing by myself would have prepared me for this.

He made his way further down, between my thighs and it made me let out a whimper of pleasure. I grabbed at his head and let his hair glide through my fingers, before latching on to a handful of it. I pulled at his hair, gently at first then with more force, pulling him into me then pushing away, I moaned a little louder this time, making him smile as he made his way back to kiss my lips.

As we both laid there exhausted from the most amazing sexual experience we both had ever encountered, I wondered to myself, were things going to be different? Of course, things were going to be different but how different? I'm not sure who fell asleep first Collin or me, all I remember is waking up the next day.

Chapter 19

Collin and I were closer now than we ever had been before. I wasn't sure how that was even possible, we already did everything together.

Now we were... Well, I'm not sure what we were. We had obviously surpassed the friendship level. We were not TOGETHER or a couple, but we were definitely not just friends anymore. I had been meaning to talk to him about what had happened that night and what it meant to him, but we just carried on as we always had.

Collin started to pressure me more about learning to control my abilities. I of course, was reluctant at first, but finally gave in, as I have said before, I can never tell him no.

I tried everything I could to move objects. I concentrated so hard that I thought I would bust a vein or something.

We were sitting at the table and Collin was coercing me to move an empty cup and slide it over to me from across the table, I stared at that damn cup so hard that I went cross-eyed. Just as I was about to give up, the cup started to vibrate.

"What did you do?" Collin exclaimed.

"I... I'm not exactly sure?" I stammered with pure amazement.

I mean yeah, a vibrating cup is not really that impressive, but at least it was something. I sat back for a moment to think about what I had done differently and couldn't think of anything, then it hit me like a ton of bricks.

"Maybe I'm trying too hard?" I blurted out.

"I don't know? How would you go about trying to not try?" Collin asked.

"Good question, I am not exactly sure of that either." I retorted.

I flopped back in my chair and thought to myself that I wanted the cup to slide across the table to me, with my outstretched hand,

I simply reached out for the cup and envisioned it in my hand, and that's when it happened, just like that, the cup slid across the table, came to a stop at my outstretched palm.

I was so elated that I couldn't even contain my excitement and Collin joined me in the jumping for joy. I had finally done it. I figured out how to move an object with the power of my mind. The feeling was so overwhelming. It was as if the weight I had been carrying around with me for months was finally lifted.

"Do it again!" Collin almost yelled.

"Okay, I'll try." I replied with equal excitement.

I again looked at the cup, willed it to come to me, it did, with much more ease this time. It was as easy as if I had just walked over and picked it up with my own two hands.

I sat the cup down and this time I slid it toward Collin. I just as easily pushed it away with my mind, as I commanded it to come to me.

"Now try something else, make it float!" Collin urged.

Okay! I thought to myself, this should be easy.

I concentrated on lifting the cup straight up this time. It started to move a little then wobbled from side to side as the plastic cup hit the table with a hollow thud and clattered to the floor.

Okay, so it wasn't as easy as I had thought to lift the cup in the air. I walked to the side of the table, told the cup to come to me in my mind, and it did just that. It zoomed from where it had fallen and practically jumped up to my hand.

I've got this, I thought to myself.

I placed the cup upright in the palm of my hand, pictured a shelf under the cup, then slowly lowered my hand. We were astonished as we gazed open mouthed at the little plastic cup, as it sat there freely floating and unmoving in midair.

We both began to laugh as the cup clattered once more to the floor. I was so ecstatic that we had finally figured out the key to my ability, but I still wondered how this was happening and why was it happening to me?

I began to move things all over the apartment now, just to see if I could. There seemed to be no limit on what I could move with the power of my mind.

We both giggled as we danced around the room ducking and dodging as objects flew around us.

I started off with smaller objects, then progressed to larger things.

First it was just little knickknacks and things. Then the bigger objects, picture frames, vases, and pretty much anything not nailed or glued down. After I was starting to get the hang of it, I could float multiple objects.

Finally, I fell to the floor, as did all the objects floating about. I felt exhausted and wasn't real sure if it was from all the excitement and adrenaline or was it from the mental exhaustion from moving things.

"What do you think this means?" Collin asked as he crawled over to where I was laying.

"I have no idea, but I can tell you one thing is for certain, our neighbors are really lucky that we live on the first floor" I added still laughing.

"No doubt." Collin agreed, grinning and breathing heavily. "I wonder what else you can do?"

"I don't know? I hadn't really thought about it. I was just happy I got a cup to move!" I said.

I laid there and thought about all the possibilities.

What else could I do? I wondered to myself.

I was excited about all the future abilities that I may discover that I have. Just when I thought I couldn't be any happier, I looked over to notice Collin staring at me.

"What?" I exclaimed. "Why are you looking at me like that?"

He was starting to make me uncomfortable, like I was some kind of freak or something.

Just as I started to speak again, he leaned over to kiss me. I closed my eyes and softly licked my lips as I too leaned toward him, I could feel his breath; our faces were so close to one another. He gently took my face in his hands and I rested my hands on his chest to balance myself. Just as our lips were about to make contact, we heard a knocking on the front door.

Collin and I just looked at each other as we wondered who would be knocking on our door at eleven o'clock at night on a Saturday, then another set of knocking, a little more persistent this time.

"Mr Summers, Mr Grainger? We know you're in there and we have a few more questions for you. It's Detective Humphrey and Detective Bishop. Open up if you don't mind." Said Detective Humphrey, grumpily through the other side of the door.

There he goes again with the IF YOU DON'T MIND, I thought to myself.

"One minute please, I'll be right there." I answered.

Collin gave me a wide eyed concerned look then just shrugged his shoulders. I stood up to walk over to the front door to let the Detectives in, I placed my hand on the door handle and paused to gather my thoughts.

Well shit! I knew it was too good to be true. They found out I had killed Paul and now they were here to take me to prison for murder!

I closed my eyes and took in a deep breath as I put on my best smile and turned the door handle.

"Detectives! How are you? What can we do for you?" I said with a little too much excitement.

"We have more questions for you, a few things didn't add up in your stories that we need to clarify." Humphrey grumbled.

"We just have a few questions for you, that's all." Detective Bishop interjected, shooting his partner a scolding look. "It's all routine, no big deal." He added with a smile as he looked around the apartment and saw the crap strewn randomly all over the floor.

"Doing a little rearranging?" Bishop said still scanning the room.

"Ha ha. Yeah, just some dusting and cleaning!" I said nervously.

"Won't you come in while we put on our shoes?" I asked them.

If nothing else I sure as hell hope we get to talk to Detective Bishop and not Humphrey, Humphrey acts like he wants to string me up or if nothing else, lock me up and throw away the key.

I swallowed hard and ushered them in.

"I'll just be a minute. Let me put on my shoes and grab my jacket. Can I offer you anything?" I asked, hoping to earn a brownie point or two.

"No, nothing. We are in a hurry and need to get back to the station. You can follow us there!" Humphrey snapped.

"No thank you." Bishop added politely, giving his partner another scolding look. "Actually, we will just wait for you two outside." He said as he all but pushed Humphrey out the door.

"Oh my god, Collin! What if they know and take me to prison?" I whispered as soon as the door was closed behind them.

"They don't and they won't." He reassured me. "Besides, if they thought for sure that you did it, they would have arrested you and not asked if we could both come to the station and not to mention it was self-defense AND even if it wasn't, how would they prove you did do it? You never actually touched Paul so who would believe that you did it with the powers of your mind?" He laughed uncomfortably as if he wasn't completely convinced himself.

I suppose that did make me feel a little better though, but I could still see us in separate rooms like in one of those cop shows on TV, where one cop slams his fist on the table and tells me that Collin has already confessed that I had done it, yet in the next room over they are telling Collin the same thing.

Yes, I know, I let my imagination run a little wild sometimes, but for real, Humphrey said that a few things didn't add up. What did that mean? Did they think one of us was lying? Oh my god! I really was going to jail tonight.

I took a deep breath in, exhaled and opened the door.

Chapter 20

We pull in to the station right behind the Detectives. The hairs on my arms started to stand on end. My mouth was so dry that it felt like I would choke. I didn't want to go in and talk to them and so much time had already passed.

Why can't they just leave it alone? Collin and I had suffered enough over the situation as is. Things were just starting to get back to normal. If learning that you had the ability to move objects with your mind, could even be considered normal! That's just my damned luck!

We walk up to the doors of the police station, PRECINCT 6 was lit up in big gold letters. As we were walking up the long row of steps, I felt like I was already walking down death row. I got the almost uncontrollable urge to run. Just turn around and run, never to look back.

Maybe Collin can talk his parents into giving us a lump sum of money and we could move to a remote island or something? Hell, maybe he could even talk them into buying us our own island? I guess that wouldn't work either, the police would be able to check the records and would just find me anyway.

Collin was obviously sensing my anxiety so he took me by the hand and gave it a squeeze. That instantly made me feel calm and safe.

"Just breathe, everything will be okay." he promised me.

I smiled back at him and squeezed his hand without saying a word and we walked through the doors together.

The precinct was just like what you would see in the movies, with desks shoved together with dividers that served as a cubicle. It was bustling for 11:30 PM, officers in uniforms were walking around and filing papers, sitting at their desks and talking on their phones.

Detective Bishop came over to show us to his office. He didn't have a little cubicle divider that was shared with another officer like everyone else. He had an actual office, on the door was lettering with his title and name.

"Detective Rylie Bishop" was printed in bold black lettering, it was very official looking.

We walked in and he ushered us to have a seat. As we sat down Detective Humphrey walked in after us, closing the door behind him and strode to stand behind the big wooden desk. It was a nice heavy looking desk, neatly organized with folder drawers and everything had it's place.

Damn! Why did he have to be here, I really disliked that man.

Humphrey just stood there and glared at me as though he really was ready to lock me up.

"Can I offer you anything?" Detective Bishop asked.

"No thanks, we are fine." Collin said in a calm easy tone. "So, what seems to be the problem?" He added.

"Well, to start." Bishop began. "It was at first thought that Paul Hill was struck by a vehicle and that's what we initially thought had killed him, but it seems that was not the case." He continued. "We have gathered further evidence that there was no vehicle involved and we were wondering if anything new had come back to either of you?"

"No, nothing at all, that I can think of? Like I said, after the bullet hit me, I passed out and don't remember anything after that. I barely remember anything prior to the gun shot either, it happened so fast." Collin told him.

"And what about you?" Humphrey said accusingly, nodding in my direction.

"No sir, nothing new at all. I'm sorry, but as I had said, I passed out too and don't recall anything that happened either. It really did all happen so fast. It's not like you ever expect something like that to actually happen to you." I told him pointedly.

"Of course!" Humphrey said disdained as he stomped toward the door. "But there is more to your story and I'll get to the bottom of this if it's the last thing I do!" He added before slamming the door behind him.

"Sorry about that. You must forgive him, he gets a little heated sometimes, but he really is a great detective and a good guy once you get to know him. He is more of an acquired taste." Bishop chuckled.

"So, Detective Bishop, if Paul wasn't ran over by a vehicle, what happened to him?" I inquired.

"We still aren't 100% sure, but I have a few theories and you can call me Rylie." He said

"If there is nothing further, are we free to leave?" Collin asked as he started to stand.

"Just one more thing before you go." Rylie said as he opened his laptop and turned it around.

There was a little window on his screen already open and you could clearly see Collin and I kneeling in front of Paul in the parking lot of Club 23.

"I got this surveillance footage from the little shop across the street and found something quite interesting on there." Rylie said as he clicked the play button.

My heart about jumped out of my chest and I stiffened. I looked at Collin out of the corner of my eye and he sat back down and didn't move.

We both sat horrified as the video played through the sequences of that night. It was as clear as day even though it was in black and white.

Damn technology! I was definitely going to go to jail now. He had solid proof that it was me that killed Paul.

I watched the short video clip with unblinking eyes, I saw as the energy flowed through my body, down my arms and out through my palms. It looked as though Paul had been struck by lightning as he flew through the air, sparks flickered to land all over the parking lot, making the camera wash out to a solid white screen for a moment.

I could feel the tears starting to form as my vision blurred and the salty tears began to flow down my cheeks.

"What does this mean for me?" I asked beseechingly.

"Don't worry, I'm the only one who has seen the footage and your secret is safe with me. Besides, it looks to me as if Paul stepped on a live wire or something. You can't really tell from the video. I guess I will just have to delete the only copy." He assured me smiling.

"What?! Why?!" Collin interjected again. "I mean thank you and I'm not trying to push our luck, but why would you do that?"

"Let's just say I know a little something about secrets." Rylie said with a smirk.

He then picked up a pen from his desk, held it in the air and let it fall. Just before it would have clattered to the desk, it came to a halt in midair, before floating over to the little cup that held other pens and pencils and turned upright and lowered in to the cup, seemingly all by itself. Collin and I just stared gaping mouths wide open in disbelief.

"How did you..." I started to say, but couldn't even finish my sentence.

Rylie just laughed and said. "You're not the only one with gifts you know? There is a whole culture out there that you don't even know about and your world is about to get a whole lot bigger. We have been watching you for some time now"

"We?" I asked in shock. "Watching me for a while? What do you mean? I just found out that night that I could even do things like that and it was totally by accident. I had no control over it. It just happened." I rambled on.

Rylie laughed again, interrupting me. "You have a lot to learn. That's how it always happens. Something traumatic happens and your abilities just sort of, awaken." He said. "That's how all telekinetics get their ability. It's always there and some get them earlier, as others get them later in life, yet some never reach their full potential, but the gene is always present, it just lays dormant until something happens to bring it out of dormancy. We call ourselves the Sais. I know that it sounds more like a college fraternity, but I guess that it's kind of like a frat. You know, being that it's such a small community and we tend to stick together.

Helping others with abilities to perfect them and get more control."

"Sais?" I asked incredulously.

"Yes, Sai as in PSI, psychokinesis." Rylie replied. "It's kind of a play on words. Plus, most telekinetics can only use our ability as a defensive tool, just like the three-pronged weapon. It's also called a Sai. No one has ever exhibited the type of power that you obviously have. That's why we have been so interested in you. There have always been sort of, legends about a 'Super Sai', but no one really believed that one actually existed, until now."

"But how did you know I even had an ability? I didn't even know I had it and what the hell is a 'Super Sai'?" I reiterated.

"You are not the only one with abilities and telekinetics are not the only abilities out there. I told you, your world is about to get a whole lot bigger. A Super Sai is someone who possesses the power to control all the abilities.

Even though it was only folk lore until now, there have always been a select few of us who believed all the childhood stories of the Super Sai, who would one day come and allow us to live in the open, but there are also those of us who still believe we should stay in the shadows of secrecy and that the world isn't ready to except us just yet. Those that believe the world isn't quite ready are the ones that sabotage anyone that tries to bring our abilities out of the shadows and in to the light" He told us sadly. "We have had our eye on you as well Collin." Rylie said almost instantly snapping back to a chipper tone.

Collin jolted up in his seat as if the chair had been electrified.

"What!? Why me? I don't have an ability and I would say that getting shot at close range is pretty traumatic!" He exclaimed.

"Your ability came much earlier than that, you just haven't fully developed it yet." Rylie told him. "That's why you two have always been drawn together. It happens naturally, our kind tends to gravitate towards one another.

You are one that got your ability at an earlier age. As I said, we have had our eye on you two for a while now. That's also why you always get your way. You can calm someone instantly from a single touch and you have the power of persuasion, the ability to make someone do anything you ask of them. Once you learn to control your ability, no one will be able to resist what you tell them to do and had you gotten to Paul and just been able to touch him, the outcome of the situation probably would have been different, but he shot you before you could get to him."

Collin and I just sat in silence. Neither of us knowing what to say. I couldn't believe what Rylie was telling us. My mind was in a whirl wind of thoughts.

"How many of 'us' are there?" I asked, still in disbelief.

"Well as I said before, it is a small community. However, there are more of us than you would probably think." Rylie told us.

"I can't believe this." I said. Talking more to myself than anyone in particular.

"Well, you are in for a treat. I know that this is a lot to take in all at once so I'll just let it sink in for a while. I'll tell you what, why don't you two go home and get some sleep and I will come by tomorrow and pick y'all up in the morning. The whole gang is very excited to finally meet you. Especially you Eric." Rylie said nodding to me.

"Me!? Why me?" I said sharply.

"Everyone is excited to meet their new leader." Rylie said matter of factly.

"LEADER?" I asked a little too loudly. "I can't lead anyone! I can barely make a decision for myself. Let alone an entire group of people. I think I'm going to be sick." I added.

"Well, sometimes we don't get to choose our destiny, our destiny chooses us and they will follow you, rather you lead them or not. So, I am not entirely sure you have a choice." Rylie said.

I looked over at Collin, who was being very quiet. I suppose he was still trying to wrap his head around the fact that he too had an ability and apparently has had it for quite some time.

We said our goodbyes and left Rylie's office, both of us still in shock. I followed Collin out of the precinct and we headed to the car to go home.

Chapter 21

On the drive to our apartment, we both sat in silence. Collin finally glanced over to me when we were almost home.

"Are you ready for this? Whatever THIS is?" He asked.

"I guess I have to be, but no. Not really." I told him truthfully.

Collin was always the one who was the leader. The one to take charge of a situation and I was the one who followed him. I am no leader, but maybe with him at my side I could attempt it. I was starting to get sick to my stomach again.

Collin took me by the hand and the sinking feeling instantly left. Maybe he really did have an ability. I just always thought it was him, not some crazy magic ability. I looked over at him and smiled.

Maybe, just maybe I could actually do this?

We strode up to the apartment door and I waited while Collin fumbled with the key, sticking it in the deadbolt and turning the key to unlock the door. I even follow with the most mundane of tasks, Collin opened the door and ushered me in.

We went in and got ready for bed still in silence. We laid there in the bed and stared up at the dark, I most definitely doubted that either of us were going to get any sleep now, so after a few hours, I just got up.

"Would you like some coffee?" I asked Collin.

"Sure." He replied in the darkness as he too got out of bed and followed me to the kitchen.

All there was to do now is wait till morning and get ready to go meet others like us.

Our kind, it seemed so odd saying it, even in my own head. Let alone saying it aloud.

I bustled around the kitchen, making our coffee.

Then I decided, since we were up, I might as well make breakfast. After we ate, we went to our bedrooms to finish getting ready.

It was going to be a long wait till it was time for Rylie to come pick us up. We were in such shock that we never even asked what time he would be here. I guess it was a good thing that we would already be up and ready for when he did arrive.

As I was putting on my shoes, I heard a pounding on the door. Collin and I both went to our bedroom doors and looked at each other from across the hall. There was a short pause then another pounding, it was a little too early for Rylie to already be here.

"Eric! Collin! It's me, Rylie. Let me in. PLEASE! I need your help." Rylie said. He sounded like it was urgent.

I rushed over to the door and opened it, just as Rylie fell in the door way. He must have been leaning on it for support. His face was all scratched up and blood was speckled all over the front of his shirt.

"We need to go, now! They are already on their way!" Rylie exclaimed.

"We need to go where? Who is on their way? What happened?" I asked with concern and panic flooding my face.

"I said we need to leave NOW!" He reiterated with more urgency.

Without another word, Collin and I helped Rylie to his feet and guided him to the car. We all but shoved him in the back seat just as a black SUV was pulling in to our complex, turning on two wheels as it sped in our direction.

"GO!" Rylie shouted.

Collin slammed the car into reverse, cutting the wheels so sharply that I bumped my head on the window as we came to an abrupt halt. Then he slammed it in drive and floored it.

The tires screeched as we lurched forward and headed toward the exit. We sped out of the parking lot like a bat out of hell and the black SUV cut sharply as it spun around and was right on our ass. We were swerving and weaving to avoid being rear ended by the vehicle.

Thank god Collin had a fast car, but the SUV seemed to be equally as fast.

They made contact with our bumper several times, causing us to nearly lose control.

"Where are you going?" Rylie asked Collin.

"To the hospital. You are injured." Collin replied keeping his eyes on the road.

"Maybe we should go to the police station instead?" I asked. "Surely they won't follow us there?"

"NO! Are you stupid?" Rylie exclaimed. Being rude for the first time since we met. "Sorry, I only mean that it won't make a difference. We need to lose them somehow." He added breathlessly.

"How are we supposed to lose them?" Collin said. "They are still right on our ass."

"I know that." Rylie replied irritated, you could almost hear the eye roll coming from the back seat. "Eric, you have to do something!" He shrieked at me.

"Me? What the hell am I supposed to do?" I asked in disbelief.

"Use your ability." Rylie said as they bumped us again.

"Use my ABILITY?" I yelled incredulously. "What would you suggest I do, throw a cup at them?" I added, a little exasperated at him for even suggesting such a preposterous idea.

"You have to at least try." Collin pleaded with me.

"Oh, not you too!" I said in return.

I flopped back in my seat pouting and concentrated on the SUV anyway. Even though I didn't really think that there was anything that I could do. I envisioned the vehicle behind us flying through the air. Then I opened my eyes and looked in the side mirror.

Nope, nothing happened, they were still closing in on us. I closed my eyes again and tried to picture the brake pedal and what it would feel like to press it into the floorboard with my mind. I peeked through one eye and still nothing.

What did they want me to do? There was a big leap from moving one little empty plastic cup, to stopping an entire vehicle.

I took a deep breath and cleared my mind the best I could. I thought back on the cup and how I had gotten it to float in midair, un moving. I had not actually floated the cup at that time, I was picturing it sitting on an invisible shelf.

It was the shelf that held the cup, not me holding the cup itself in my mind's eye. Just then, they bumped us again, making the car lurch then weave from side to side.

"I don't know how much longer I can keep doing this?" Collin said looking at me with pleading eyes.

I didn't say anything. I just closed my eyes and thought about the SUV hitting a low, but thick concrete wall.

I felt my body tingling and the smell of electricity like ions filled the air. The hair on my arms stood on end and with every part of my being, I pushed the wall out of my mind as if willing it into existence.

Just as the SUV was about to rear end us again, the front end crumpled as if hitting the invisible concrete wall and the vehicle flew into the air as it summer salted end over end and rolled to a stop behind us.

"WOOHOO!" We all three shouted in unison, celebrating our victory.

"Oh, my god! You did it! You actually did it!" Collin shouted elated.

"I knew you could do it!" Rylie said to me with more energy now.

I whipped around in my seat and glared at him.

"Who was that and why the hell were they after you?" I exclaimed. Demanding an answer from Rylie.

He instantly stopped smiling as if I had slapped him with my words.

"It wasn't me they were after." He said grudgingly. "They were after you, Eric." He added, as he looked down to his lap as if to avoid eye contact.

I didn't say a word, I just turned back around and stared blankly out the windshield.

"Where are we going then?" Collin asked Rylie. Purposefully changing the subject.

"Take a left up here. I'll tell you were to go." He replied without inflection.

Collin slowed the car down to a normal driving speed and followed Rylie's directions from turn to turn. As we drove down the streets, I halfway expected Rylie to lead us out of town to some off the beaten path country road or to some mysterious, creepy looking house out in the middle of nowhere or if nothing else to an ominous bat cave or something cool like that.

That didn't seem to be the case, with each turn we took, the buildings just got bigger and nicer. I was really shocked when he had us pull in to some gated, security controlled parking garage.

Rylie handed Collin a black credit card sized object from the back seat and as Collin held it up and turned it over to examine it, I could see that it was a keycard.

"Just hold it out the window at the call box and the gate will open." Rylie told him.

Collin did as he was instructed as he rolled down the window and held out the keycard to the little grey box planted right outside the car, with in a second, the gears started whirring and the metal gate clattered and shuttered as it began to lift open. Collin gave me a disconcerting glance, I could only return the same look.

Chapter 22

Even as nice and well-lit as the parking garage was, it still let off a very ominous vibe.

The huge multileveled parking garage was enormous and as we looked around, there wasn't a single vehicle to be seen. I think that is what was putting off such a malevolent feeling.

A huge garage completely vacant. It was like staying overnight in a dilapidated mansion that didn't have one thread of furniture or decor. It just wasn't right and it gave me the willies.

"Drive up to level 3 and park by the elevator and we can take it up from there." Rylie said while pointing in the direction we needed to go as if there were another way to get to level 3.

As we rounded the corner of level 2 and came up to level 3, we noticed all the cars parked in rows. At least now it seemed to be a little more welcoming. All the cars ranged from old beat up clunkers to very expensive imports.

We parked the car by the elevator as instructed and Collin and I got out of the car, I opened the back door for Rylie as Collin walked around the back, to help me get him out.

He seemed to be doing a little better, but he still had blood seeping through his shirt. I just realized that I had never even asked Rylie what had happened or why he was injured. Rylie was wearing regular street clothes and I don't think that I had ever seen him in anything other than his uniform. He was even more attractive in regular clothes than I thought he was.

He caught me looking him up and down and I quickly glanced down at my feet, embarrassed that I had been caught, my face flushed with red as the blood rushed to my cheeks.

"What? I can't help that I am bleeding." He said with indignation. "I'll pay to have your car fixed AND cleaned!" He added with an even more resentful tone.

I suppose he was still mad at me for accusing him of being the reason we were chased down in the first place, so I didn't tell him what I was really thinking.

"I am not worried about the car. We need to get you to a hospital." Collin told him.

"No, I'm fine and there is someone here that can help me. We just need to get to the top floor." Rylie said.

As we made our way over to the doors and pushed the button that would bring the elevator down. Rylie began to sway back and forth just as the elevator dinged and the doors opened. We walked in all but dragging Rylie with us.

"Press the button for level 21 and use the keycard to activate the doors." Rylie told Collin.

Collin retrieved the black keycard from his shirt pocket, pressed the button for level 21 and inserted the card into the slot.

Almost immediately, the doors closed and the elevator began the ascend to the top floor. My heart was racing as we neared the top. I had no idea what to expect or what would be waiting for us when the doors opened.

Hell, I wasn't even completely sure we could trust Rylie. After all, we didn't know him from Adam, I suppose we were just happy that we may finally get some answers about what was happening to us.

It hadn't even crossed my mind that there might be an army of government agents or something, just waiting to take us hostage as soon as we reached the top floor.

Once again, the elevator dang and my stomach churned. I was so glad that I had not eaten too much for breakfast or I would have for sure lost it.

The doors opened and we stepped out into the lobby. To my surprise, there were no agents waiting to pounce or men in masks waiting for the doors to open.

No men with guns drawn and running towards us shouting to get on the ground. It was nothing like what I was expecting, there was a huge circular receptionist desk directly in front of us and rows of offices on either side and to the back of the desk was a huge glass wall that had a spectacular view of the city and long corridors that lead to the left and right of us.

"Rylie! What happened?" Exclaimed the woman from behind the desk as she rushed around and ran straight to him.

"Nothing Love. I'm fine, just a few bumps and bruises. I just need to see Doc." He told her calmly.

"You've been shot." She said, almost in a whisper.

I stiffened.

Shot? Did she just say that he had been shot? How did I not notice that?

Now I felt even worse for treating him the way I had in the car.

"I'm fine Tina, really I am. Doc will fix me right up, no worries." He reassured her.

"This way! Follow me!" She exclaimed, with more urgency.

Collin and I did as instructed and followed Tina down the long corridor to a double door at the end, with Rylie in tow as Tina burst through the doors and held one open for us to bring Rylie in.

"Over there, on the table!" Tina ordered, pointing to a large stainless steel table with medical equipment lined up against the wall.

This was obviously used as some kind of operating room or a makeshift clinic if nothing else. It all seemed to be a little more hi-tech then I was expecting. Then again, I didn't know what to expect about anything, so I don't know why I was surprised.

She ran over and picked up the intercom, pressing a few numbers and shouted in to the receiver.

"Doc! We need you in the medical bay immediately!"

Tina didn't even give the person on the other end a chance to reply before she hung up the phone and rushed back over to Rylie, taking him by the hand.

"I told you not to go, that something bad was going to happen." She scolded him gently, finally starting to calm down a little.

"And you know that I had no choice. They were going to kill him." Rylie said

"What! Kill who?" Collin said, speaking for the first time.

"They were after Eric. They would have killed you both had I not gotten to you first." He told us, then continued. "As I was on my way to get you, they tracked me down and I tried to lead them off so I could get to you first, but I wrecked my car when they shot out my tires. So, I ditched the car and headed to you on foot. I was hit by a stray bullet and I'm still not completely sure how they didn't find you first, with me being on foot. They must have not known exactly where y'all were yet?"

The look of shock and panic ran across my face.

"Why would they want to kill me? I haven't done anything." I said dumbfounded at hearing that someone was trying to kill me.

"And besides all that, how do they even know about Eric?" Collin asked with despair forming with each word.

"The same way we knew about you two. I can sense when a person's abilities awaken and I know how, when and where to find them. Not always, but sometimes I can even sense before an awakening." Tina interjected, answering for Rylie.

The doors swung open, slamming back against the wall with a clap. The bang scared the hell out of Collin and me both, but our nerves where a little on edge at the moment.

The man that came bursting through the doors was a younger man, maybe in his thirties. However, he had flecks of prematurely graying hair that sparkled like glitter as he rushed over in our direction.

"What happened?" Doc asked, ignoring everyone but Rylie.

"I was shot by the Mansfield Group. They were on their way to capture Eric and I intercepted them before they got to him." Rylie told him nodding over to me.

Doc cut the front of Rylie's shirt with a pair of sterile medical shears, revealing his rippled abs and a tribal tattoo of a sun on the left side of his chest.

Doc ran his hands above Rylie's wound.

"You're lucky this time. The bullet has gone all the way through. We should have him up and running in no time." Doc smiled at Tina.

Collin and I watched in amazement as Doc closed his eyes and rubbed his hands together. As he did so, the energy produced by his hands began to light up, forming a brilliant blue orb as he separated his palms. It seemed to just float there in midair as he pushed it down and into Rylie's gunshot wound.

It instantly began to close and heal as if it had never happened. The sweat on Rylie's forehead began to subside and color returned to his cheeks. He sat up and rubbed the spot where the bullet had entered.

"Dang Doc! You're getting good. Not even a scar this time." Rylie told him jokingly punching his arm.

"Well it was nothing. Just a flesh wound, really. Actually, I'd call it more of a scratch. You're just a wuss, crying over a little bullet wound like that, it barely grazed you." Doc joked back.

The two laughed thinking their jokes were funny, obviously the three of us were lost on their little comedy routine, as none of us laughed along.

"Oh, I almost forgot. This is Eric Summers and Collin Grainger." Rylie said pointing to each of us as he said our names.

"And this is Roger Cryton, but we call him Doc for obvious reasons." Rylie smiled as he pointed a thumb over his shoulder at Doc.

Collin and I just nodded at Doc, still flabbergasted at the events that just took place.

"And you already kind of met my wife, Tina." He said holding out a hand for her to come over to him.

She was still not smiling and looked irritated with Rylie as she walked around the table to take his hand.

"So, would y'all like to meet everyone else?" He asked, unfazed by her disapproval.

"I would like to know what the hell is going on!" Collin said in reply.

"Okay, okay." Rylie said chuckling, holding his hands up as if in surrender. "Let's start with that, but first I need to eat. I'm starved. Anyone else hungry?" He asked as he jumped off the table and headed to the exit without looking back, putting his arm across Doc's shoulders as he lead him out and they joked and laughed some more.

If looks could kill, then Rylie would have fell over dead right then and there. All three of us shot him dirty looks as we watched them stride out of the room like nothing ever happened.

"I'm really starting to dislike that man. It's a good thing I love him." Tina said, more to herself than to us, as she too headed toward the exit.

Collin and I looked at each other and grinned. I think the feeling was mutual.

"We are finally going to get some answers at least." Collin told me as we too headed for the exit.

"I am not completely sure I want to know the answer?" I said, only half joking.

"Well come on. Something is better than nothing." He replied.

Then we ran to catch up to Tina and she smiled as we caught up.

"I hope you boys are ready for this." She said with eagerness.

"Ready for what?" I asked grudgingly.

"Just wait and you'll see." She replied with a smile that made me even more uneasy.

Chapter 23

We followed down a long corridor to another set of double doors. As we walked through the doorway there was a huge open room with rows of tables set up and chairs down both sides of the tables.

It reminded me of a school cafeteria. The blue and white tiled floor was laid out in a checkerboard pattern and the fluorescent lights overhead seemed to buzz and flicker as they came on.

I looked around for Rylie and Doc who were nowhere to be seen. Tina sat down at a table near the front of the room, which I assumed was closest to the kitchen.

"Come have a seat." She told us as we went to sit beside her.

A few moments later Doc and Rylie came out of the kitchen with sandwiches and drinks. They came over and sat at the table, placing a plate in front of each of us.

"Okay, what would you like to know? You can ask me anything." Rylie said.

"We would like to know everything." I told him, still a little irritated.

"Well if I told you everything, we would be here for a while." Rylie chuckled.

"Start with who the hell was trying to kill me and why." I said pointedly.

Rylie shifted uncomfortably in his seat and picked at his plate. "They are called the Mansfield Group. They are the ones I was telling you about yesterday. The ones that don't want our abilities to come out in the open. If the rumors are true and you really are a Super Sai, they will stop at nothing to get you on their side. If they can't persuade you to join them, then they feel they have no other choice, but to kill you. They know about you, the same way we did. Tina has the ability to kind of sense when a person's abilities awaken and she can tell what ability they will have." Rylie said.

"But still, I don't understand. Why does everyone think that I am this Super Sai? I can just move things and nothing else." I said, looking to Rylie.

"I had never felt anything as strong as that night when you stopped Paul, the feeling was indescribable. It woke me out of a dead sleep and I'm sure I am not the only one who felt the surge. That is a lot more than just moving things, it takes a great deal of power to produce that kind of energy. That's why you passed out, your body wasn't used to handling that kind of power drain. Your abilities are like a muscle and they have to be conditioned and worked out, just like any other muscle." Tina interjected.

"As I said yesterday, most of us only have one ability and it takes a great deal of strength to maneuver small objects, let alone to take someone's life or to stop a moving vehicle dead in its tracks." Rylie said with conviction. "And you seem to be able to do those things with ease. It takes years for some of us to develop our abilities and it takes a great toll on the body to move even small objects." Rylie continued.

"So how do the abilities work? Where do they come from?" Collin asked, speaking for the first time since we entered the cafeteria.

"No one really knows for sure how they work, just that they do. The gene that suppresses our abilities, for some reason is weaker in some people and just snaps, causing our ability to awaken. Everyone has the gene, but no one knows why we have it, or why only some of us get abilities. There is a theory that as humans we continually evolve and that it is just something nature has given us as a defensive weapon. Others theorize that we are all a government conspiracy, part of a scientific experiment gone wrong." Doc chimed in.

"There are many abilities out there. Most of us have the ability to move objects like me. Some can heal like Doc while others have premonitions like Tina and some are even powerful enough to have the power of persuasion like Collin." Rylie added.

"Power of persuasion?" Collin reiterated.

"Yes, with a single touch, you can make someone feel at ease or fear their own reflection. After time and a little practice, you will soon be able to do it without even touching them and you will be able to make people do whatever you want.

Some can fight the urge of compulsion, but most find it difficult, if not impossible." Rylie told him.

Collin just stared at him blankly as if he were speaking another language.

"What does this mean for us now?" I asked.

"You can't go home, that's for sure. Mansfield obviously knows where you live now. It won't be safe for you there." Rylie told us.

"What do you mean? We can't just, not go back home. We have our own lives to live and we have school." Collin said still in shock over what we were just told.

"Well what good is going home or school for that matter, if you're dead?" Doc asked rhetorically.

"Surely they won't kill us?" I asked, more as a statement than a question.

"Of course, they will and they will stop at nothing until you either join them or you're dead. The Mansfield Group is a menacing people. They will kill you without thinking twice and they will do whatever they can or need to do, to keep our abilities a secret."

"I don't understand why they want me dead so bad. What does it matter if I join them or not? Maybe I could just go and talk to them, tell them that I won't tell anyone about us." I said.

"They have an agenda and if you don't fall within their parameters, then you are of no use to them and they have no problem disposing of anyone who gets in their way. You could go talk to them, but you would probably never be heard from again." Tina told me with a sadness that shown all over her face.

It was if there was more to the story and they weren't telling us everything.

"What about this building?" I asked. "Who pays for all this stuff?"

"We have our ways." Rylie chuckled. "There are others that have joined us that are like Collin. They get big Corporations to 'donate' funds to us." He continued.

"That's stealing!" Collin exclaimed!

"Not exactly," Doc chimed in again. "We just use a bit of persuasion to push them in our direction. It's not like we are robbing them and besides all that, they get to use it as a big tax break.

So technically, we are doing them a favor." He laughed.

"Well that's one way to look at it as the glass is half full." Collin told him, still frowning.

"I guess I'm just stupid, I still don't understand." I said. "Even if I am this Super Sai, that doesn't mean that I will go and tell the world about our abilities and it doesn't mean that I will be able to lead anyone. Like I said before, I can't make my own decisions, let alone make them for anyone else."

"Well, the story goes that there will someday be someone that will have abilities so great that they will have the power to control all abilities and they will bring our people out from the shadows and into the light, that we will be able to openly use our abilities to help others and make the world a better place. That's the short version anyway." Rylie told us.

"What would be so bad about that?" Collin asked. "Why would anyone with abilities want to have them kept a secret?"

"Dr. Mansfield used to lead our people." Rylie began. "My mother and father were part of his team.

I grew up watching him do great things for our kind and at one time we thought him to be the fabled Super Sai, but the power got to his head and he became someone we didn't recognize. He began to think of our kind as a superior race, that the people without abilities needed to be eradicated. He could never control all abilities, but he could control several. He figured that it would just be a matter of time before he could control them all. My mother and father tried to stop him and he killed them, after that we broke off into two groups. We have done everything that we can to put a stop to him, but he always seems to get the upper hand and escapes. As of now, no one has had the power to stop him once and for all. We are hoping that you are that person, Eric."

"Okay, enough of the macabre stories for now." Tina told Rylie. "Why don't you take the boys down to meet the rest of the team and give them a tour of our facility?"

Rylie smiled and nodded. "Okay then, y'all ready to see the rest?"

Collin and I stood with Rylie and silently followed him as he led us out of the room.

Chapter 24

We made our way back to the elevators and took it down to the 11th floor. It's hard to take in all the information that was just given to us.

What were we supposed to expect? These people wanted me to be their leader and I wasn't even sure if I wanted to be, or even could be their leader?

It was both frightening and exhilarating to think about finally being around people like us.

I looked over at Collin, who seemed to be in a trance.

"Are you okay?" I asked him and he stiffened as if I had just slapped him.

"I'm not sure yet!" He said, his voice seeming to tremble.

"It'll be okay." I told him. "We will figure things out."

The elevator dang and the doors slid open, we stepped out into a huge open room. There were pool tables and arcade games on either side of the room and a huge red leather U shaped couch was in the center of the room.

"This is our common area." Rylie told us. This is where we come to just unwind a bit if we need to.

There was an old-school jukebox playing some rock song, but the volume was too low for me to tell what was playing. The jukebox was like one of those old timey retro ones, with the neon lights that had bubbles scrolling around the trim.

There were two people over in a corner occupying a pool table. Rylie led us over to where they were, they stopped playing their game and just stared as we walked over.

"Hey Bridgette, hey Carl, I'd like you to meet Eric and Collin." Rylie said as he introduced us to them.

"Hello. I'm Eric and he's Collin." I said meekly.

Bridgette smiled at me and offered her hand for a shake.

"Nice to meet you." I told her, as I too extended my hand.

"This is Carl." She added, giving him a nudge to say hello.

"So, you are the infamous leader, huh?"

I heard a voice that seemed to be coming from everywhere, but no one had said anything.

"Speak aloud please." Rylie told Carl.

"If he can't even communicate with thoughts, how is he supposed to be the all mighty leader?" Carl scowled, as he threw his pool cue on the table and stomped out of the room.

"Sorry about that." Bridgette told us, he gets a little short tempered sometimes.

"What was that all about?" I asked.

"He just lost his brother, Jade to the Mansfield Group and he's still upset. He is just taking it out on you because you're new. He didn't mean it. We aren't sure if Jade is still alive or if they killed him. They captured him a couple weeks ago when Jade and Carl were out on a mission." Rylie said.

"That's terrible." Collin said, finally speaking.

"Yeah, it is, but we will get him back, if he's still alive." Bridgette said with such sorrow.

"Bridgette, I have to run an errand, do you mind showing the boys the ropes? Maybe show them where they will be staying?" Rylie asked her.

"Not at all. It would be my pleasure." She said.

Rylie left us in the care of Bridgette, as he headed back toward the elevators, just before the doors closed, he gave me a reassuring smile.

So far, I liked Bridgette, she seemed to be nice or at least she was nicer than her friend Carl, but I suppose I can understand why he may have been a little disgruntled, I would be devastated if I had lost Collin.

"So, what would y'all like to see next?" Bridgette asked, clapping her hands together.

After Bridgette gave us the grande tour, she took us back down to the 10th floor.

They had made this floor apartments for people like Collin and I, who had nowhere else to stay.

When we walked in to apartment number 12, there was nothing fancy about the room, it reminded me of a hotel room. I think at one time these all used to be separate offices.

There was a little kitchenette as soon as you walked into the room that had a mini fridge, an electric burner for a stove and a microwave.

The bedroom and living room where combined by a couch that folded out to a bed.

I wasn't looking forward to staying here and was definitely going to miss our bed at the apartment, at our home, not this place.

Bridgette had assured us that we would be given better accommodations if we were to stay there for an extended amount of time, but she said that we may be able to go back home soon, so I was hoping that she was right.

We just had to wait till they made sure it was safe for us to return.

I was just glad that I was finally alone with Collin, I had been wanting to talk to him about everything since we had arrived here.

"What are you thinking?" I finally asked him as we were unfolding the couch to get some much needed sleep, after we had a sleepless night last night.

"I'm not really sure exactly what to think." He told me.

"Everything is going to be okay, at least we are safe and together." I said.

I wasn't sure whom I was trying to convince more, him or myself.

"How can you say that?" He asked with trepidation.

"Well obviously, I have no idea what's going to happen, but I'm just trying to stay optimistic." I told him.

Our roles were reversed, it was always him that was trying to convince me that things would turn out okay. I wasn't very good at doing the whole, everything's going to be okay attitude.

"Hey, look on the bright side, you said you wanted an ability and now you know you have one." I said, trying to make light of the situation.

"Yeah, I guess." He said with melancholy.

"Once you learn to hone your ability, people will do whatever you tell them to do, that's pretty damn cool, a lot better than just moving things around!" I said, trying to sound excited for him.

"I think I'm just really tired and need to get some sleep." He said with a halfhearted smile.

"Okay, me too." I agreed.

We laid down and got under the covers together as Collin held me till I fell asleep.

Chapter 25

I woke to an alarm blaring and the only light was coming from a red flashing emergency light strobing overhead Smoke was starting to fill the room and I shook Collin in a panic to wake him.

"What the hell is going on?" He said as he jumped to his feet.

"I'm not sure, but we need to find Rylie!" I exclaimed.

We threw on our shoes and rushed to get out, at least we fell asleep in our cloths last night and were already dressed.

Collin and I ran to the door and as Collin flung it open, smoke billowed into the room and started choking us instantly. Collin slammed the door closed and ran over to the kitchen sink, grabbed two hand towels and soaked them under the running water.

"Here, use this for your nose and mouth!" He shouted as he threw me one of the damp towels.

I was in a panic, I wasn't sure what had happened or what the hell we were going to do now, we rushed back to the door, covered our mouths as Collin opened the door again.

We ran down the hallway to the elevators, trying to stay low to keep the smoke to a minimum.

"I think we should take the stairs!" Collin suggested.

I just nodded as we burst through the stairwell door. We took the flight of stairs up to the next level two by two, the smoke was not as thick in the stairwell.

The door to the Common Room was jammed, I was in such a panic that I didn't even have to think about it.

I pushed my hands out toward the door and used my mind to pop the metal door off its hinges, the door folded as if it were made of foil and burst through into the Common Room flying to the middle of the room.

Collin just looked at me, but there was no time to waste. We rushed through the doorway, only to find an empty room.

"We don't have time for this and we can't search the entire building, we need to get out!" I told Collin, as I took him by the hand and all but dragged him back into the stairwell.

We were leaping down the stairs as fast as we could, but going down two by two steps was a little harder than going up them.

We were already half way down, almost to the parking garage, when out of nowhere someone was chasing us down the stairs.

"Wait! Stop!" The stranger shouted after us.

Collin and I came to a halt on the landing to wait for him to catch up to us.

"Hey! I'm glad I finally found you." He said as he was bounding the last few steps to catch up.

He was wearing a red hoodie and had a bandana covering his mouth and nose.

I could see him smiling from the corner of his eyes and just about the time I was going to return the smile, my body started to tingle, again warning me that something just wasn't right.

"Eric! Collin! Get away from him! Run!" I heard Bridgette yelling from behind me.

I turned to look at her, the fear and panic she had on her face sent me in overdrive.

I looked back in the stranger's direction and he was standing only a few feet away from us. He had his hands shaped like he was holding an invisible basketball, only instead of a basketball, there was a glowing red ball of fire.

He drew his hands back as if he were about to fling the ball directly at me.

Again, I reacted as if by instinct, I brought my hands together and forced them outward with everything I had, the energy flowing through me like it had with the door.

The hooded stranger flew through the air slamming against the wall with a thud, knocking him unconscious.

"What the hell! Who was that?" I exclaimed.

"That would be Jade Red, Carl's brother." She told us, pulling both of us by the arms and leading us back down the stairs.

"He must be with the Mansfield Group now. You are lucky, he is one of the most powerful Sais we know. He could have really hurt you two, or even worse, killed you." She said, not slowing down.

"At least Carl will be glad to know his brother is still alive." Collin said.

"True but we can't worry about him now, we have to get out. The Mansfield Group has taken over and set fire to the building. Most of us have been captured and there are only a few of us left. We have to get to a safe place, then we can regroup!" Bridgette shouted.

"Where are we supposed to go?" Collin asked.

"I'm not sure yet. Just give me a minute to think. Right now, we just need to get to the parking garage." She said all flustered.

"Collin's parents have a lake house just outside the city. Do you think we could go there?" I asked.

"I don't see why not. No one should be there this time of year." Collin said.

"Great! Let's get the others and we can go there!" Bridgette said with elation.

CHAPTER 26

We made our way down to the parking garage and there were five people already standing around, waiting for our arrival. I looked around the otherwise empty garage, I couldn't see Rylie anywhere.

"Where's Riley and Doc?" I asked Tina who had obviously been crying.

Dr Mansfield and his team took them with the rest of us." She sulked.

"I'm so sorry!" Collin and I said in unison.

"What does this mean?" I asked.

"Will they be okay?" Collin interjected.

"We don't know anything yet, but again, we can worry about that later, for right now we need to worry about ourselves and get to safety!" Bridgette cut in.

"Where should we go?" Tina asked Bridgette.

"Collin said his parents have a lake house, we should be safe there, until we can come up with a plan to get everyone back from Dr Mansfield. It'll be okay, we WILL get them back!" She told Tina.

"Okay everyone, you heard her, lets load up." Carl said, talking to everyone.

Without another word the eight of us got in two separate vehicles. Bridgette tossed Collin a set of keys.

"Collin, you drive and Tina, you follow us." She ordered.

Bridgette, Carl, Collin and myself all piled in to one SUV, while the other three got in another vehicle with Tina and we headed out of the parking garage and got on to the highway.

The lake house was about an hour drive outside the city, it was a beautiful property and best of all, it was private and secluded.

As we drove further into the country, the trees got thicker and the road narrower. We pulled off the highway and took a caliche road, for what seemed to be forever, before turning on to a dirt road that lead up to the lake house.

It was a cabin style home with all the amenities, of course. I had only been here a few times, but it was still a place that made me feel safe, it felt like a home away from home.

We made our way down the dirt road to a gravel drive and came to a stop in front of the house. It was a two-story cabin style home, and had a rustic feel to it.

Collin's parents hired landscapers to maintain the property and the maids still came to clean, when it wasn't in use, so it still looked as though someone lived there. We would have to figure out how to keep them away for a while, or at least until we figured where and what we were going to do.

We got out of the car and walked up to the huge wraparound porch that had an old wooden swing that hung by chains from the rafters, while Collin went over to where his parents had hidden a key and went to unlock the door for us.

The interior was just as pristine and manicured as the outside, the furniture and décor matched the rustic motif.

"Everyone make yourself at home." Collin said as we all piled in the front entryway.

"Someone needs to make a supply run." Carl stated to no one in particular.

"We can go together, there's something we need to talk about." Bridgette told him.

I assumed she was wanting to tell him that his brother, Jade was still alive and that we had seen him, but I didn't want to be part of that conversation. She was going to have to tell him that he had tried to kill us and had apparently decided to join the Mansfield Group.

We didn't really get a chance to talk on the way over here, everyone just sat in silence and stared out the window. I think mostly, we were all just in shock that our world seemed to be crumbling down around us and we couldn't seem to catch a break, especially Collin and me.

As Bridgette and Carl prepared to leave, to go get food and supplies, everyone else started to settle in and make themselves a little more comfortable.

Collin was trying to be as hospitable as he possibly could, given the situation.

He was organizing sleeping arrangements and gathering things together that we may need. He was going around collecting towels and toiletries for the bathroom, grabbing extra blankets for those that would have to have a makeshift bed and extra pillows.

He really was a sweet guy, the way he cared for others. I thought as I watched him bustle about the lake house.

Even as precarious as our situation was, I couldn't help but to smile. He could always make me smile, even when he didn't know I was watching him.

Bridgette and Carl finally returned with food and other supplies, I for one was grateful, I was starving and was sure everyone else was too. Collin showed them to the kitchen, as I went to put things away and help him cook dinner for everyone.

"What do you think will happen now?" I asked Collin after everyone left the kitchen and we were alone.

"I'm not really sure?" He told me.

That was a little disconcerting to me, Collin always knew what to do.

"Do you think we will be able to get Rylie and the others back safely?" I asked.

"I don't know Eric, why are you asking questions that you know I don't have the answer to?" He scolded.

"I'm sorry." I said. Sulking and looking at my feet.

"No, I'm the one that's sorry!" He said, lifting my chin with his fingers, making me look him in the eyes. "I'm just a little stressed out and I don't mean to take it out on you."

"It's okay." I reassured him.

"No, it's really not." He said.

Then he pressed his lips to mine, his action took me by surprise. I wasn't expecting him to be so intimate, when someone could walk in on us at any time, but I didn't care, I leaned in and returned the kiss. Collin slowly leaned back and smiled at me.

"It's all going to be okay, we will get a game plan together and get the others back. I don't know how, but we will get them back. You'll see, everything is going to be just fine." He told me.

I didn't know how, but I believed him when he said we would get the others back. It was just a gut feeling I had and I knew it was true. We would do anything and everything in our power to get them back, safe and sound and I knew everything was going to be okay or at least that's what I hoped.

Look for THE PURGE BOOK TWO, coming soon, to find out what happens next.

Will Eric and Collin prevail and be able to save their friends from the Mansfield Group? What other abilities will Eric find out that he has? Will he and Collin be able to overcome the stresses of their new life on the run and be okay? All that and more, to come in the next installment. I hope you have enjoyed

THE AWAKENING BOOK ONE
BY J.R. HASTEY

J.R. HASTEY